Elin's Island

Elin's Island

Cynthia L. Copeland

The Millbrook Press
Brookfield, Connecticut

Published by The Millbrook Press, Inc.
2 Old New Milford Road
Brookfield, CT 06804

Library of Congress Cataloging-in-Publication Data
Copeland, Cynthia L.
Elin's island / by Cynthia L. Copeland.
p. cm.
Summary: Thirteen-year-old Elin can't imagine living anywhere but the
island off the coast of Maine where her father is lightkeeper, until the night
in 1941 when she awakes to the sound of German torpedoes while her parents are on the mainland.
ISBN 0-7613-2522-0 (lib. bdg.)
[1. Lighthouse keepers—Fiction. 2. Islands—Fiction. 3. Rescue
work—Fiction. 4. World War, 1939-1945—Maine—Fiction. 5. Interpersonal
relations—Fiction. 6. Maine—History—20th century—Fiction.] I. Title.
PZ7.C78797   El 2003 [Fic]—dc21   2002007205

FOR MY MOTHER AND FATHER.
WHEN I AM WITH THEM, I AM HOME.

Chapter 1 ⌒

. . . In the first three days of September, 650,000 children were evacuated from London alone. Hitler had stated that his war would not be waged against women and children, but in Poland, no one was safe from the bombs being dropped at his orders. The British were not going to risk the lives of their children. So youngsters from four to sixteen were rounded up from cities thought to be potential German targets and taken away in carts, by bus, and by train, headed for the safety of the countryside. They stood in crooked queues, wearing ID tags, clutching suitcases and the compulsory gas masks, waiting to be evacuated. Weeping mothers, who were forbidden to see them off and were not told where they would be taken, stood consoling one another outside the railroad stations . . .

Bang!

Elin was startled out of the newspaper as Andrew exploded through the kitchen door and slammed it behind him. He planted a can of oil at his feet.

"Whew!" he said, shaking himself like a wet dog. The chilly gust that followed him in sent the seagull hanging by the window into a lazy spin.

"Hello, Franklin!" Andrew hollered at the wooden bird. Andrew had bought him at the general store on the mainland and named him after the president. He always greeted the bird first.

"Quiet your voice, Andrew," Sarah said from where she was stooped over the coal stove. "You're not shouting over the surf now." She turned with a frown, but smiled as soon as she saw him. "You're wetter than a bucket of water!"

Andrew wiped rain from his eyes with hands red and raw from the cold, then tugged at the knot under his chin that held his hood in place. He struggled for a minute, then managed to untie it.

"That's some storm brewing out there," he said, stomping his boots on the mat. "Blew up from nothing out of nowhere." He paused as if impressed by the storm's ability to sneak up on him unnoticed. "Didn't expect it. Thought the wind would die down by midday, but I'll tell you, that sea is roaring and lunging like a lion on a leash."

He began to unbuckle his raincoat. "Yup, it roars and lunges but always retreats. Trust the fellow who's holding onto the other end of the leash, and when the beast is agitated, admire it from a distance."

"Like a lion on a leash," Elin said quietly. She liked the sound of that.

"Any damage to the light?" Sarah asked.

"Not yet. And none to the boat, either. Anything that might get blown about I put in the boathouse and—" He pointed at Elin. "Your chickens are back in the coop."

"Thanks, Andrew," Elin said.

Sarah nodded and went back to poking at the coal in the stove with a shovel, trying to coax out a little more warmth. "Our coal stores are low," she said into the orange glow. "I didn't expect we'd have such cool weather in August."

"That's what makes living on an island in Maine so interesting—you never know what the weather will be like the next day or the next week," Andrew said. "No need to worry too much, Sarah. We'll talk to the Coast Guard supplier after the storm. And we have plenty of wood." Andrew pulled back his hood and his red hair stood up like the comb of a rooster. Elin giggled. He shed his coat and hung it on a peg. Then he came over to the table where Elin was reading. Leaning his big frame forward, he gave her a chilly hug and rubbed his wet beard against her cheek.

"Yuck!" she said.

"What?" he asked in mock surprise. "I'm just hugging my conscientious daughter who remembered to read those newspapers for her current events quiz."

"Some of these papers are from 1939—almost two years old, did you know that?" Elin struggled to free herself from his damp embrace. "How come you're making me read old ones?"

"I'd been saving certain papers for a time so you could read about the war in Europe, the important events, when you were old enough to understand. I want you to know what's happening over there, especially now, with the war spreading."

"But it's all happening so far away." Elin continued to squirm. "What does it have to do with me? Except for my quiz. You are going to quiz me, right?"

"That's right darlin', I am. Twenty questions on what's in those articles, with one jelly bean for every correct answer." Andrew straightened up. "And it really isn't as far away as you'd like to believe."

Elin pretended to shake the water out of her dark braids and slunk down in her seat. She looked at him in dismay. "Twenty questions? That's too many. We'll never have time to play checkers before dinner if—"

Andrew stopped her with his raised hand. "Twenty questions. In fifteen minutes." He turned and leaned toward Sarah. "Have you had a chance to look at the papers from last week? It's hard to believe all the horrors going on over in Europe right now—" He shook his head and sighed. "Well, anyhow, I'm going to change out of these wet things."

He stomped off toward the bedroom, whistling the same tuneless song he always did. Elin heard him say, "Brrr!" as he stepped beyond the stove's circle of warmth.

"That's why I'm reading in here!" she shouted after him. "Every other room in this house is like an ice box!"

"That's the great thing about living in Maine—"

"I know, I know!" Elin interrupted him. "You never know what the weather's gonna be like!"

"Hey, who's my little smart aleck?" Andrew shouted back from the bedroom.

"You know, it would be a lot more peaceful around here if you two could carry on a conversation in the same room," Sarah said, still pushing the coals about. But she sent a smile in Elin's direction.

Elin tried to concentrate on the newspaper, but the storm was too interesting to ignore. She peered out the window into the gloom. She could feel the coldness slipping into the house through invisible cracks in the wall. Rain pounded against the glass in a random pattern, sounding like the beat of a beginner's drum. Elin tried to tap her fingers to the uneven rhythm. Dumdedumdumdum . . . dumdumdedededum . . . .

Even though it was an hour or more until nightfall, the natural light filtering through the window was dim. Elin took down the kerosene lamp that hung near the stove, filled it from the oil can Andrew had brought in, and lit it. She carried it to the table and set it near the pile of papers. The dark print leaped off the page in the circle of light.

Elin pushed through the pile of old papers to the ones at the bottom that she hadn't read yet. It was hard for her to believe that Sarah had let Andrew keep newspapers for so long. She usually swooped down upon anything that would burn and fed it to the fire.

At dawn on May 10, 1939, German paratroopers dropped on Holland. At the same time, Hitler's gliders flew over the Belgian side of the Albert Canal, and within minutes the important bridges were taken by the Germans. The glider troops dropped explosives down the gun turrets of Fort Eban Emael, spreading flames and gas throughout the fort. Holland surrendered in four days . . .

Andrew reappeared in dry clothes.

"Don't you think you should light the lamp in the tower now?" Elin asked. "It's real misty."

Andrew stared out into the rain for a few minutes. Then he turned to Elin. "C'mon, El. Help me get things going up there."

"You mean I can stop reading now?"

"For the time being."

Elin pushed the papers to the middle of the table. She loved to be invited into the lantern room. Up there, feeling more like part of the sky than the earth, she and Andrew would share secrets as he polished and painted. They'd talk about mermaids and sea monsters, about pirates and ship-wrecks and sunken treasures. Just two years ago, Andrew had said she wasn't old enough to help. But now he knew that she wouldn't scratch or bump into anything.

She grabbed her sweater from the peg next to the door, slipped her feet into her work boots, and followed Andrew out the door that led to the passageway.

The kitchen was attached to a long, low shed that led to the lighthouse. They called it the passageway and were lucky to have it. Lots of other keepers had to fight through fierce weather to take care of their duties in the tower. Andrew had added two small windows a few years back. When the angle of the sun was just right, Elin could hopscotch in the squares of light that shone on the rough, wooden floor. Not today, though. The murky grayness coming in the windows barely lit their way to the dark rectangle that was the doorway to the lighthouse.

Elin's black dog, Sailor, thumped his tail in greeting from where he lay near the end of the passageway. He didn't bother to get up or even lift his head. Elin reached down and rumpled the fur behind his ears.

"Thanks for letting him in, Andrew," she said. Sarah had strict rules about the dog and where he was allowed to be. Never inside the house—too much dog hair. If the Inspector were to make a surprise visit and find dog hairs strewn about, that would surely mean a black mark. Elin and Andrew had an unspoken arrangement, though. One of them always let Sailor into the passageway when the weather was particularly bad.

"Good old boy," she said, smoothing the damp hair on his back. "I'll bet you'll be glad when this storm is over so you can go out and chase the chickens."

Sailor's tail thumped a reply.

Andrew bent over to grasp the can of oil that he filled each morning and put at the base of the lighthouse stairs for the night. "Elin, be a good girl and run back for the lantern."

She dashed back to the kitchen and then caught up with Andrew on the fourth step. He reached back for the lantern and sent a glow ahead of them. The flickering light painted spooks on the wall that darted and danced with each of his steps. The round walls distorted the light, pulling and stretching their shadows into eerie shapes. Elin stayed just one step behind Andrew, careful not to kick the toes of her boots against the white risers. If she marked them up, she'd have to repaint them.

She always counted the stairs as they climbed, without thinking about it. There were fifty-two. Last year, Andrew had taught her to count in French, probably because he was tired of hearing her count in English.

Vingt-huit, vingt-neuf, trente. She followed his steps, around and around and around, higher and higher. She barely heard the hissing of the lantern over the surf's roar. The waves hit the rocky shore with the sound of a cannon's boom, then retreated and attacked again. She could feel the excitement rising inside her, but she could not let it show. A storm was serious, and it was never good news for anyone at sea. But drama on the island was rare and hard to dislike.

"Who said, 'I have nothing to offer but blood, toil, tears and sweat'?" Andrew called back to her.

"Andrew!" Elin said. "It hasn't been fifteen minutes and I'm not done studying!"

"Well?"

"Churchill. Winston Churchill, but don't ask me anymore."

"And he is the . . . ?"

"This is the last one, Andrew. British Prime Minister. Now don't ask me any more until I've finished studying!"

"Last one, but it's tough." Andrew paused for effect. "Who is Joseph Dzhugashvili?"

"Aaaandrew, that's way too hard!"

"All right, I'll give you another one. The answer to that

one was Joseph Stalin. He made himself absolute dictator of Russia in 1924 after whose death?"

"Lenin?"

"Correct. Now get this one and we're done until after dinner. What does the German word *blitzkrieg* mean?"

"Oh! Something about war . . . like a storm or . . . I know! Lightning war!"

"You're right! Very good!"

With relief, Elin noted the final steps before the first landing. No more questions for now. From the first landing, a ladder took them to the second landing and another ladder led to the lantern room. Just a year ago, Andrew had made her go first, in case she needed a push from behind, but now she was old enough to take care of herself. He only glanced back quickly at the top of the second ladder to check on her. He pushed the hatch open with his head.

"Fingers off the brasswork," he said as he lifted himself into the lantern room.

"Andrew, you don't have to tell me that every time." Elin closed the trapdoor behind her.

One of the windows was hinged like a door, and it opened onto the gallery, the narrow deck that encircled the tower. Elin began to undo the latch.

"It's much too windy, El," Andrew said. "You'll be blown right off."

"No, I won't." But she redid the latch and surveyed the sea through the glass.

Andrew pulled the cloth bag off the lamp, revealing the sparkling reflectors. He filled the small reservoir tank on the back of the lamp with enough kerosene to feed the wick all night, then flipped the tank upside down into its holder. He lit the wick and brought it to its lowest point.

Then he put his finger in the flame and brushed off the burned ends. Once he leveled the wick, it would burn evenly.

Elin peered into the mist. Her eyes knew every bump on the horizon, every ledge that ominously surfaced at low tide. She took slow steps around the room, her eyes focused on the crazy waves. The white tips were barely visible in the rain-drenched fog. She had nearly completed her circle when she noticed something unfamiliar in the water. She picked up the binoculars Andrew always kept in the tower and focused on the smudge. She could make out something that looked to be a white patch of sail and the shape of a boat tipping to one side.

"Andrew, look at this," she said, handing him the binoculars.

"Boat's taking on water, all right," Andrew said, frowning into the glasses. He stared for a few long seconds while Elin waited. The best view was from up here. At sea level, it would be impossible to see anything at a distance.

"I'm guessing they're nearly a quarter mile out, to the north . . . northwest, more like." He continued to stare through the binoculars. Then, suddenly, he set them on the floor.

"Good eyes, kiddo," he said with a grin. "Let's go rescue somebody."

"I can go?" Elin asked, her green eyes wide.

"You're the one who spotted the boat, right?" Andrew was already halfway down the first ladder with the lantern. Elin scrambled after him. She swallowed a few extra breaths to feed her pumping heart.

As they stampeded down the tower steps, Elin sent Andrew a silent thought. If he asked Sarah's permission, she'd surely say no. She was such a worrier.

He had to avoid going into the water himself. Drowning people were desperate and often pulled rescuers under with them, even strong swimmers like Andrew. He'd told her that last year after another rescue. Suddenly, Andrew shut down the motor and grabbed a small paddle from under his seat.

"Wait for my instructions," he said over the wind. "And then toss those. Throw them in *front* of anyone in the water."

"*Me* toss them?"

"When I say so."

Andrew was using the paddle, first on one side of the boat with a few strokes, and then on the other, to maneuver near the sinking craft. As they lurched about on the waves, he stared at the black water.

Now it loomed before them—a long, fancy sailboat, polished wood with painted trim that seemed to reflect light even in the gloom. A cabin rose from the sloping deck, and the endless mast tipped toward the waves. The sail had been dropped and lay in folds that flapped in the wind. But there were no signs of people.

Elin's forehead wrinkled in concentration as she stared into the dark turmoil of storm-tossed waves. Were they too late? Had she spotted the boat too late to save anyone? Andrew fought the swells and paddled closer to the boat, then turned to circle it.

"Hey!" he shouted. "Hello! Please respond!"

They strained to listen over the ceaseless wind but heard nothing. Elin felt tears rising to mingle with the raindrops and sea spray.

"Hey!" Andrew shouted again. The storm gobbled up his words as soon as they left his mouth.

All at once, the sky let go. The wind drove into their

boat, and the drizzle grew to pounding rain. Elin rested the life preservers on her knees and pulled the sides of her hood against her cheeks. Each pellet of rain bit hard at her face and hands. She suddenly realized how cold she was and felt her body shaking in an attempt to fight off the chill. Andrew paddled hard on the right side of the boat to force it to turn against the waves and then paused. He reached between his feet for the lantern and held it up. The haze sent the rays of light back to them, making it even harder to see.

"Hello!" Andrew called.

This time Elin thought she heard a muffled reply. She turned quickly toward Andrew. He nodded. He'd heard it, too!

He dropped the small paddle and grabbed the oars lying in the bottom of the boat. Sliding to the middle seat, he slipped them into the oarlocks. He turned his back to Elin and began to row with purpose, working around the drowning vessel, digging deep into the waves to propel them forward.

As they rounded the tip of the boat, Elin half stood to get a better look. Andrew must have felt her weight shift.

"Sit, Elin, sit!" he commanded. Elin quickly dropped back down and held a life preserver up, ready for his instruction. Andrew powered a few more strokes, then allowed the waves to shove him toward the craft.

"I'm going to jump onto the deck," he shouted back at Elin. He seemed to be developing the plan as he was talking. "You're going to have to do the best you can to keep our boat close, without hitting the sailboat. Don't let the waves swamp you."

Elin dropped the life preservers and twisted completely around to grab the oars as he released them. She felt where his hands had been, where the wood was warm and dry. She held one out, shoving it against the slick side of the sailboat to keep the boats from colliding.

Andrew picked up the life preservers, thrust them high on one arm, and shifted the swaying lantern into that hand. He stood on the seat, balanced precariously. A giant swell brought the swamped side of the sailboat within reach and he pulled himself up with his free hand.

"You can do it!" he shouted to Elin and then scrambled onto the deck of the sailboat and dropped into the cabin. Elin moved to the middle seat for better control of the oars. She pushed off from the sailboat and rowed with all of her strength against the tempestuous sea. As she worked her boat a short distance away from the other, the sea continued to batter it without mercy. She stared hard at the sailboat as she fought the waves, watching for Andrew to reappear. But it seemed as if the harder she stared, the less she could see. The details of the sailboat were swallowed by the mist and darkening skies and her own blurry vision. Soon, only its ominous shape remained.

She continued to pull in rhythm, forcing her vessel to make a laborious circle around the drowning boat. Delving deep into the swells, Elin felt the muscles in her arms straining. She pulled the oars into herself, then let out a breath as she brought them back for another pull. Pull, breathe, pull, breathe.

She tried to ignore the water dribbling into her eyes. As she twisted around to keep the sailboat in sight, the wind snatched off her hood, giving the rain an easy path down the back of her neck. But she didn't interrupt her rhythm. Pull, breathe, pull, breathe.

Where was Andrew?

Each time the sea attacked, Elin fought back, working the oars hard as she strained to look for Andrew. Then, there he was! Elin could make out the faint light from the lantern arcing in the distance. She fought with renewed vigor against the swells.

As she neared the sailboat, Elin saw two people with Andrew. She was surprised at how young they looked. One was probably a teenager, the other looked even younger. Under their life jackets, their clothes clung in wet folds to their skin. The smaller one hung onto Andrew with desperate arms.

"Hurry up!" he yelled, his voice shrill with alarm.

Elin maneuvered her boat alongside the sinking vessel. She could see that it had taken on more water since Andrew had boarded.

"I'm going to get in first!" Andrew's voice boomed over the breaking waves. "You boys hang on right here, and then I'll help you into my boat." Andrew let himself into the back of the motor boat while Elin steadied it as best she could. He half-crouched as he prepared to help the boys down.

"Dan, you first," he called out.

The bigger of the two boys slid down the sloping deck. Andrew reached up to guide him. Just as his feet landed next to Andrew, a swell lifted the boats high and then dropped them, yanking them apart. Dan and Andrew fell to the bottom of the boat. Elin struggled to keep the sea from claiming the oars. Don't let go, she told herself. Don't let go!

Andrew pulled himself to his feet and pointed. "Sit over there for weight," he commanded. The boy stumbled past Elin to the bow seat.

Elin could hear the other boy hollering. "We're coming!" she shouted to him.

She worked the left oar to push closer to him. All at once, she saw him leap off the deck and disappear into the

The boat rolled over the swollen waves. The drone of the motor filled in when the voices stopped.

"How did you know we were drowning?" Jack asked weakly.

"I saw your boat from the tower," Elin said.

When he looked puzzled, she added, "Lighthouse," and pointed to the beam.

"Who's going to be worried about you two?" Andrew called out.

"Our folks," Jack said. He sounded as if he might cry again. "But they won't even know we're gone until morning. We lied and told them we were staying overnight at Jimmy's. He's our cousin."

"I'm afraid we have no way of contacting your parents tonight," Andrew said. "But we'll head to town first thing in the morning, all right?"

Jack nodded and leaned closer to his brother for comfort. Dan rested his cheek briefly on top of Jack's head. She couldn't tell whether the misery on both of their faces was from the cold or from fear of the punishment that would likely face them when they returned. Dan would get the brunt of it, she reasoned. He looked old enough to know better. He was probably older than she was.

When she realized she had been staring at him, Elin felt her face redden. She looked beyond him to the lighthouse. Its powerful beam sliced through the mist, guiding them toward the island. Squinting against the spray, she watched as it grew brighter. The boat rocked with the swells, struggling toward the dock, heading for home—for a seat by the stove, for dry clothes and a cup of hot cocoa. And maybe even for a scolding from Sarah, for taking such a risk. But the scolding would only last a few minutes, and the memory of her first rescue would last forever.

Chapter 2 ⌒

ELIN WOKE TO sounds of barking. Often at dawn the seals fought over the rocks that surfaced as the tide pulled out. The largest rock was the grand prize and the cause of the noisiest battles. One old gray seal usually managed to flop on top of it and keep the others off, though they would bark at him from their lowly rocks long after his victory had been secured.

She smiled, thinking of them out there yelping at one another, noses upturned, whiskers poking out from either side of their enchanting faces. Once she had found a baby seal alone on the island's southern beach. She had taken it back to the house, intending to keep it in a big tub and raise it as a pet. She even knew what she would name it—Magnifique, after the boat that had been shipwrecked on the island hundreds of years before. Manny, for short. But Sarah had made her bring it back to the rocks and let it go.

The pale light of daybreak slipped through the windows of Elin's bedroom and stole away the night blackness. The storm clouds had moved on and taken the rain with them. The wind had calmed, and now it blew simply to urge the waves onto the shore. No longer in chaos, the surf had returned to its rhythmic pattern of tumbling in and retreating.

Elin pulled the blanket over her head to stay enveloped in darkness. She relished this time, these few moments of being awake but not busy, of dreaming and dozing in the fuzzy pre-dawn, before time started pushing her through her daily duties. She was free to lounge until she smelled the morning breakfast smells and heard the noises of a new day beginning.

It soon grew stuffy under the covers, and so she re-emerged. Lying still, she gazed at her walls with sleepy eyes. Her room was tucked under the roof, with sloping walls that felt close and snug. Sarah, whose taste ordinarily tended toward the plain, had taken a sponge coated with very light pink paint and made a pattern on the walls. Around the windows and door she had painted dainty roses, pink and red, with bright green leaves. Even though these were not on the list of regulation colors, the Inspector had never mentioned it in his reports. He had overlooked it, either by accident or on purpose, every time he came, and the roses had stayed for twelve years now.

Elin tried to pretend that she didn't hear footsteps in the living room, then in the kitchen. The murmur of voices. Laughter. As the drowsiness left her, Elin remembered their guests. She heard Andrew's low, rumbling voice mingled with Dan's, then Jack's urgent exclamation. More laughter.

Now the stove cover made a scraping noise as Sarah slid it aside. Rattle, rattle, ca-chink, ca-chink. She was shaking the grate to make the ashes that had gathered throughout the night fall into the bin below. Elin pulled the pillow around her ears so that she could barely make out the sound of coal spilling into the hole to resuscitate the few remaining weak, red chunks. More voices, more shuffling footsteps. Sizzling and snapping as slices of bacon were dropped into a hot pan. It was easier to ignore the sounds than the smells. The sweet, salty bacon smell and the scent of coffee brewing snuck under her door and demanded attention. She could resist morning no longer.

Getting out of bed was like going swimming. The cold was a shock, but it was best to get it over with quickly. She always dove right into the cold water from the dock, and now she tossed the covers back all at once and leaped for her bureau. She yanked open a drawer. Shivering in the unheated room, she stripped off her nightgown and then pulled on dungarees and a shirt, then a sweater. She walked into her slippers and charged for the stairs. Sometimes it amazed her that summer days could start off so chilly.

She scooted through the living room and burst into the kitchen, eyes fixed on the stove where the coal hissed and the bacon still crackled. Sarah was busy, her back to Elin. Andrew leaned heavily against the kitchen counter, sipping black coffee and studying last week's newspaper. He frowned and shook his head, then folded up the paper and tossed it next to the stove.

At the table, Dan and Jack hunched over plates over-flowing with food. They were dressed in some of Andrew's clothes, their own still too wet to wear. The sleeves of the flannel shirt Jack wore were rolled up in thick cuffs, and a belt cinched tight held up the baggy borrowed pants. Dan, who was a good deal bigger than his brother, didn't have to make quite so many adjustments. He had cuffed the pants, but his broad shoulders filled out Andrew's shirt. His hair, which had been matted to his head the night before, had dried light brown and curly. He was probably sixteen, or maybe even older.

Elin opened her mouth to say "Good morning" as she always did, but something about having strangers in the kitchen made her hesitate.

"Hello, sleepyhead," Andrew teased.

Elin blushed as she slipped a plate out of the cupboard and focused on the stove.

"The boys were just expressing their thanks, Ellie," Andrew said, "and I told them to save it until you came down. You deserve a lot of the credit."

Elin smiled briefly in Dan's direction.

"Really appreciate the help," he said. "I couldn't fall asleep last night thinking about how close we both came to . . . to . . ." He forced himself to finish the sentence, "drowning."

"That's our job," Elin said. The words sounded more severe than she meant them to be. She concentrated on holding her plate still as Sarah served her bacon, eggs, and pancakes. She thanked her mother, slipped into the seat across from Dan, and set her plate down too hard. Sarah startled at the clatter.

"Oh, sorry," Elin said.

"You planning on coming with me to town today?" Andrew asked her. "We'll return Danny and Jack and bring in some of my paintings to the store. You feeling up to that?"

Elin glanced anxiously at Sarah, who was bustling about as if she hadn't heard, consumed with the task of feeding breakfast to twice as many people as she normally did. If Elin was gone for most of the day, Sarah would have to do her share of the housework.

"If Sarah doesn't need me to help around here, I could come," she said. Sarah continued flipping pancakes and stirring scrambled eggs and fried potatoes in concentrated silence. Elin wasn't sure if she hadn't heard or if her silence was tacit approval.

"I'm sure it'll be fine." Andrew continued making plans. "We won't be gone long, and the weather looks good. Can't smell any fog."

Dan looked up from his plate. "How's that?"

"When you've been out here as long as we have, you can smell fog long before you see it," Andrew explained.

Elin leaned over to take a bite of her pancakes, and she paused, letting the steam and the sweet smell of maple syrup wrap around her face. She took a long breath and then stabbed her fork deep into the stack of pancakes. She chewed just enough so the food wouldn't choke her, then went in for another bite, and another.

"My goodness, slow down, child, you'll get a stomachache," Sarah chided as she set the coffee pot on the table. Elin stopped mid-chew and felt her face turn hot.

"I know why you're so hungry," Andrew said. "You fell asleep before dinner last night. You were exhausted."

"I am very hungry," Elin offered weakly.

"Me, too," Dan said. "And I have no excuse. I did eat dinner last night!"

"Well, you're a growing boy." Sarah dumped another stack of pancakes on his plate. "You need lots of food to keep your energy up."

Andrew gestured toward the table. "Finish up, everybody, so we can get on our way." His gaze fell on Jack's plate. "What's going on there, buddy?" he asked. "Don't you like your breakfast? Sarah's the best cook on the whole island, you know."

Jack gazed forlornly at his plate of food and poked at the eggs with his fork. "With my mom's eggs, you can see the white part separate from the yellow part," he said as if he were talking to the eggs themselves.

Sarah turned from the stove and smiled at him. "These are called scrambled. Your mama's eggs are fried. Would you like me to make you some fried eggs or—"

"He's fine, really," Dan said. "This is delicious." He

leaned close to Jack. "You'll see Mom real soon. Just get something into your stomach, okay?"

Jack nodded and nibbled on the edge of a pancake.

Dan finished what was left on his plate and refused thirds. He took his plate and coffee cup to the sink. Elin's gaze stayed on him as he washed and dried them.

"So, you didn't sleep too well last night then, Dan?" Andrew asked.

"Well, I think I was just feeling pretty awful about what happened," Dan said. "That was probably the dumbest thing I've done, especially because I had Jack with me. It could have been . . . ." He trailed off as his voice wavered. In a minute he added, "And then, of course, I lay in bed listening to the waves." He shook his head and managed a grin. "They're so loud! I'm just not used to listening to crashing waves out my bedroom window."

"What do you usually hear at night?" Elin's curiosity won out over her shyness.

He sat back down at the table. "Oh, I fall asleep to crickets chirping, coyotes howling far off, the sheep annoying each other in the barn, sometimes the neighbor's dog. Things like that."

Elin considered this as she took a bite of her egg. "I just can't imagine it," she said.

"I can't imagine living out here all the time," he said, then quickly added, "I mean, it's just so different from the way most people live."

"It's a wonderful place to live!" Elin declared. "And by keeping that light going we save lives every day! Every single day," she added for emphasis.

"But what about friends? Kids your own age? I mean, it's just you and your folks out here. What about school and dances and movie dates and things like that? You must be, what, thirteen or fourteen?"

"Thirteen. Fourteen in a few months. How . . . how old are you?"

"Fifteen," Dan said and, as if he anticipated the response, added, "I'm big for my age. Now, at thirteen years old, don't you wish for a little more excitement sometimes?"

Sarah turned around, her spatula poised in mid-air, as if waiting to hear Elin's answer.

Elin frowned. She scraped the last bit of egg from her plate and stood up to clear her place. "We have plenty of excitement here," she said. "Why, when I was five, there was a shipwreck on the southern reef. And once it rained for twenty-two straight days! And then there was the time three years ago when we had two goats that wandered out onto a sand bar and nearly drowned when the tide came in."

"A real shipwreck?" Jack said. "I wish I'd seen that!"

"Wasn't yesterday's enough for you?" Dan smiled ruefully at his brother.

"It can be a little monotonous," Sarah admitted as she set down the spatula and wiped her hands on her apron, "especially for a young person. Except for things like storms and visitors like you boys, it can be hard to remember what was different about last week, or last year."

"That's right," Andrew said. "Now you're our new marker. Like, 'a week after we pulled those boys in' or 'twelve days after the boys sunk their boat' . . . like that."

"Terrific," Dan said and groaned.

"I wouldn't mind living here," Jack said. "No neighbors to yell at you when you ride your bike across their lawn. You could go fishing whenever you want and, hey! no school, right? You don't have to go to school!"

"You have a bike?" Elin asked. "Is it hard to ride a bike?"

"It's not hard." Jack waved his hand in exaggerated bravado. "I ride my bike everywhere."

watched the ship surrender to the storm and sink. And then Andrew spotted something through the lens, something bulky rising and falling with the giant waves.

"He hurried down the rocky slope and waited for the thing to wash within his grasp. When at last he could drag it out of the raging surf, he found that it was a feather bed, tied with twine."

At this point, Andrew always picked up the story.

"It was heavy," he said. "So it was a bit of a struggle to carry it inside. Expecting to find a ship's log or perhaps jewelry or family heirlooms, I unwrapped it on the kitchen table. Tucked inside the feather bed was a box. And when I opened the box, I found no jewels, no captain's diary. I found a baby. She was silent, wide-eyed. She was cold, but she was alive."

"I hurried to wrap the infant in layers of blankets," Sarah continued. "Andrew and I simply couldn't understand how she had made it to the island. We were stunned. How could a baby be unharmed by the same storm that had brought down a mighty ship? This tiny bundle should have been swallowed by the waves or blown into the open sea. But washed into the arms of a couple who had lost their own daughter just three months before? How?"

Sarah paused so that the miracle could be fully appreciated. Elin glanced at the boys. They were both watching Sarah intently. Jack's mouth hung open slightly.

"The baby's mother must have seen our fire," Sarah went on. "Certain the sea would claim her life, she had hoped against all reason that it would spare her child. What prayers must have passed over her lips as she placed the bundle upon the churning waves? There was no time for her to write a note, or maybe no words to tell all that needed telling."

Now it was Elin's turn.

"The baby from the sea grew up to be me," she said. "Because no one from the mysterious schooner was ever found, Andrew and Sarah adopted me. They called me Elin, after Sarah's mother, her guardian angel, she says. And I've always called them Sarah and Andrew, because that's what they call each other."

"So that's why you call them by their first names!" Dan exclaimed.

Elin shrugged. "Why not?" she said. "We celebrate my birthday on the day the storm brought me to the lighthouse."

"Don't you ever wonder who your real parents are?" Jack asked.

"Andrew and Sarah are my real parents," Elin answered firmly. "Oh, sometimes I wonder about the mother who tried to save my life, what my father looked like, my very first name. But I don't have any question that this is where I belong. I was meant to grow up here. With these parents. Daughter of a lighthouse keeper. It's just that it took an act of God and nature to bring me to the right place."

Dan had been watching Elin intently since she began her story. She met his gaze and quickly looked away. But out of the corner of her eye, she could tell that he continued to stare at her.

"Are you going to live here forever?" Jack asked, his eyes round.

"Forever," Elin answered. "This is my home." She saw Sarah and Andrew exchange glances, and added, "I could not live anywhere else. I've told Andrew and Sarah that many times."

Elin stood up and walked quickly out of the room without looking back.

Chapter 3

As their boat neared the coastal town of Rock Point with the boys on board, Elin felt the familiar rush of excitement mixed with anxiety. What would the day bring? A day in town was always something different, not like a day on the island. There would be faces she'd never seen, smells that were unusual enough to merit attention. There would be voices other than Andrew's and Sarah's. There would be someplace to spend her twenty cents! She reached into her pocket to be sure the dime and two nickels were still there. And then, late in the afternoon, just as she'd had her fill of crowded stores and strangers, there would be the familiar ride back to the island, where Sarah waited with bowls of fish chowder and warm biscuits. It would be an interesting day, no question.

She twisted about in her seat so that she wasn't staring directly at Dan and Jack. Out of the corner of her eye, she thought she saw Dan staring at her, but she quickly shook off the idea.

They were close enough now so that she could see the church spire rising from among the far-off hills. She could even count the windows in the grand houses that overlooked the sea. The windows were like eyes, soaking in the view of the vast ocean. Houses competed for space along the water's edge, with only the rare mansion having enough room for a tree or a row of hedges to separate it from its neighbor. It made Elin feel lucky to have a view of the ocean all to herself from everywhere on the island.

As Elin rubbed her coins against one another, she looked toward Rock Point Harbor. It was enclosed by great man-made piles of stone that were like giant arms reaching from the shore. The hands didn't meet; they left just enough room for two boats of good size to pass by one another upon entering or leaving. Entering the cove felt like slipping into an embrace.

To the right, a peninsula jutted into the water at one of the giant's shoulders. As they drew near, Elin saw a crowd of people assembled at the very tip of the land. Sometimes a few people would gather just to take in the sight of the open sea, but this was more than a few. Elin strained for a better look, narrowing her eyes to try to bring them into focus. These were not people from town, she knew that right away. Nor did they look like the tourists who swarmed the place during the summer months. This group, over-dressed in somber clothing, appeared to be waiting for something, most facing toward the open sea.

"Wonder what all that commotion is about," she said to Andrew, pointing so that even if he could not hear her well over the motor, he would understand.

He squinted at the distant huddle and shrugged. "The fishermen have all gone out by now," he shouted to her. "I don't know what's going on."

Elin looked quizzically at Dan. He, after all, had been on the mainland just yesterday. She and Andrew hadn't been for over ten days.

But he raised his eyebrows and shook his head. "No idea," he yelled.

The motor boat slipped through the opening, and Andrew eased up so that the boat was crawling. With the motor quietly sputtering, Elin could hear the gulls laughing and crying as they circled the harbor.

The tide was out, and the great rock walls halted the waves, making the water in the harbor remarkably still. The air, too, was quieter here. American flags hoisted from the beach houses floated rather than flapped. The still air felt damp and smelled strongly of seaweed and fish waiting to be taken to market.

Now Elin could see that the crowd consisted of men in hats and dark coats. None of the men working on the docks wore hats, unless it was to keep off snow or rain. As the boat moved slowly by the peninsula, Elin noticed cameras on tripods set up near the water. Some of the men had books or notebooks tucked under their arms. Maybe a fishing boat was lost or had capsized! But she couldn't imagine why even that would draw such a large crowd.

Andrew guided the craft around the sailboats anchored in the middle of the harbor. There were many tied in place, dormant sails wrapped tight, masts stretching so high it was as if each was trying to outdo the other. Most were covered with brightly colored tarps to keep off the rain.

"It's as if they're patiently waiting for a bright Sunday afternoon so that they can glide out toward the horizon," Elin said. Then she realized that no one knew what she was talking about. "The sailboats, I mean," she added.

Jack sat upright. "Won't be long now!" he sang out. "Look, Dan! We're almost home!"

Dan groaned and hunched over in his seat. Chin cupped in his hands, he stared out at the water. His gaze lingered on each sailboat they passed.

"That one is about the size of my uncle's," he said glumly as they hummed by an impressive white boat.

As Andrew steered around a sailboat named *Maribelle*, Dan said to no one in particular, "My uncle's was called *Dolly's Delight*. Dolly's my aunt."

Elin tried to think of something to say that might make him feel better, but she couldn't think of anything. If he had been Andrew or Sarah, she would have reached over and put her arms around him. Just the thought made her blush.

"So, Dan," Andrew said in a cheery tone, "you're just about the same age as my nephew, Ted. You know a boy named Ted Whitcomb?"

"Oh, sure, I do!" Dan's grimace turned momentarily to a smile. "Ted and I have been buddies since we were five or six."

"Well how about that!" Andrew said. "How about that, Elin?"

Elin smiled politely and nodded. She didn't think too much of cousin Ted, with his bragging, know-it-all manner.

"Rock Point's not such a big town," Dan said. "Most of the kids know each other, at least enough to say hello."

"Well, that's true," Andrew said.

Dan's smile faded as he settled back into his anxious thoughts.

~ ~ ~

A sliver of land split the harbor in two and sent out wharves like branches into the water. Each was lined with fishing shanties and decorated with random sculptures of worn-out lobster traps heaped high. Because it was low tide, seaweed climbed the piers that propped up the docks and crawled over the rocks that had surfaced near the water's edge when the sea flowed out.

Andrew veered to the left. As their motor boat droned by the first long wharf, Elin looked back at the crowd still gathered. She watched until the boat rounded the end of the wharf and they disappeared from her sight.

Andrew did not have his own spot, so he would have to find a place to tie the boat at the farthest dock that was tucked under the massive stone wall that rimmed the harbor.

"There's a space!" Elin called out. Andrew cut the engine and picked up a paddle. The boat had no neutral or reverse gear, so he had to take care that he did not slam it into the dock. The boat drifted slowly in, urged ahead by the slightest of waves.

Andrew put the paddle out to prevent the boat from hitting hard against the pier. He guided the craft with the paddle until it was bobbing gently next to the dock. Elin leaped out and pulled the bow of the boat against the nearest post. Before she could reach in for the rope, Jack was standing up and stepping toward her.

"Careful," Andrew warned.

Jack balanced in the middle, hesitant to step out. Elin leaned forward and offered her hand. He waited just a second or two, then took it, letting her yank him onto the wharf. He let out a whoop and began bounding down the worn boards toward the ladder that climbed to the top of the stone wall.

"Thanks, Mr. Whitcomb," he called back. "Thanks, Elin!"

"You're welcome, Jack," Andrew said.

"Thank you," Jack called again, waving the bag that held his wet clothes like a heavy flag.

Elin flipped the rope around a sea-beaten post and tugged the knot tight. When she stood, she saw Dan with his hand out, waiting for hers. She reached out and pulled him onto the wharf. He didn't let go of her hand right away. She slipped out of his grasp.

"You're pretty strong for a girl," he said, managing a smile.

"For anyone," she said.

"True," he said.

He grabbed his sack of clothes that Andrew had tossed beside him.

"Thanks, both of you," he said, "I, uh, I don't even know how . . . "

Andrew waved off his gratitude. "Just go and tell your folks that you're safe," he said. "That's going to be the most important thing to everyone."

"Right," Dan said. He nodded. "Right," he said again, as if to convince himself.

"I'll be seeing you," he said to Elin.

"Okay," Elin said, although she couldn't imagine where.

He set off after his brother, the wharf shaking under his heavy stride.

"Wait, Jack!" he called out.

Elin watched until they had both hauled themselves up the ladder and disappeared over the top. Then she turned to Andrew.

"You'll probably never see those old clothes again," she said as she caught the other rope he tossed and tied a quick knot.

"Sure I will," he said with a grin. "And I'm hoping those nice boys return 'em in person so we'll have another visit with them. How about that Dan? He's a handsome young fellow, don't you think?"

"Oh, Andrew," Elin snapped. Jamming her hands onto her hips, she frowned down at him. "Why would you think

I'd notice a thing like that or even care! I mean, why would I care about seeing Dan again? Honestly!"

But Elin wondered for an instant if she would ever see him again, not because she felt a fondness for him or any such silly thing, but to find out what his parents did to him when he got home. And maybe to visit him, to see what kind of house he lived in with coyotes in the woods and sheep in the barn. There were a lot of things she was still curious about.

"Ellie!" Andrew broke into her thoughts.

"Hand it up." Elin leaned forward and took from Andrew the canvases stretched tightly on wooden frames and set them at her feet. As she pulled the paintings up, one or two at a time, she examined them with the scrutiny of an art critic. First, two paintings of sunsets, then one of the lighthouse at dusk, and three of the waves curling into the rocks on the beach. They were familiar; she had watched him create them all, usually in his favorite spot at the base of the tower, sheltered somewhat from the wind.

She paused at the next one, holding it up for inspection. "Andrew, I've never seen this one."

Andrew squinted up at her. "What's that?"

"This painting. Of me standing on the gallery. When did you paint it?"

Andrew stood up. "Oh, when you weren't paying attention to me, Rapunzel," he teased. "You were pretending to let your hair down for the prince to climb up."

Elin blushed. She told herself a lot of stories when she looked out from the gallery. Andrew had captured a moment when she was dreaming about being somewhere else, and someone else. She was leaning forward in her baggy overalls, letting her long braids hang over the railing. The wind was pushing the bangs away from her face.

Andrew had even painted the brown flecks in her green eyes and splashed freckles over the bridge of her nose. She admired the painting for several minutes, then added it to the stack.

"I really like it," she said. "It looks just like me. That's the first time you put me into one of your paintings."

"I guess I couldn't bear the thought of selling my Elin to some strangers from the city." He smiled up at her.

"Oh, but now you can?" Elin said.

Andrew chuckled as he handed her two more—one of Sailor sitting on Shipwreck Point and the other of a bucket of fish and a fishing pole. The boat empty, he hopped with ease onto the dock. He picked up some paintings with each hand and tucked them under his arms. Elin took the rest. Then they followed the weather-worn wharf to the ladder.

Elin set down the paintings and stepped over the water to the bottom rung of the ladder and nimbly pulled herself up. At the top, she turned and got down on her hands and knees, lifting the paintings up one by one. When Andrew had passed her the last one, he hoisted himself to street level.

They each carried several paintings as they hiked along the narrow piece of land that divided the harbor. On the other side of the inlet were fishing boats at rest. Elin often considered the contrast between the sleek weekend sailing vessels on one side and these dingy fishing boats, reeking of old clams and pleading for paint, on the other. The fishing boats, she had decided, led a more interesting and useful life. If she had to be a boat, she would be a fishing boat, smelly or not.

She and Andrew walked side by side until the point of land opened up onto Main Street. When they turned right,

Elin felt the hug of the narrow street lined with stores and restaurants. Suky's Sweets held its breath next to the Hull House Restaurant, which nearly leaned against Yolanda's, a boutique that sold fancy clothes to the tourists. Between Yolanda's and Helmet's Strudel was barely room for a shaft of sunlight. The doorways of every building encroached on the street like an over-eager crowd at a parade.

But Elin noticed the colors more than the closeness. Bright flowers overflowed from window boxes and road-side barrels and pots. Wreathes of dried flowers decorated nearly every door. Though the buildings were sided with shingles that had weathered to gray or brown, the shutters and the trim around the windows and doors had been painted with gay pastels. Awnings of aqua and rose and daisy yellow shaded the windows. These were colors, Elin thought smiling, that would make the Inspector shudder!

Today the dirt road was congested with men dressed like those on the peninsula, milling about aimlessly. Bicycles rolled along, bells jingling to announce their approach. Horses pulled carts full of vegetables to the store or packages back home, and a few shiny automobiles chugged by.

"Newsmen," Andrew said as he strode toward Stan's General Store. "These fellas are newsmen. Must be something important to bring them all here."

"You think they heard about our rescue yesterday?" Elin asked as she ran a few steps to keep up with him.

Andrew laughed. "I don't think so. And anyway, I don't suppose more than one or two local folks would be interested in that story."

As they walked along, Elin peered into the windows. Tip Top Toys had a train set that zipped along its oval track past miniature buildings and people. In Kate's Gift Shop, where Andrew always bought Sarah's Christmas present, rings and bracelets and necklaces sparkled on a fisherman's net, and the Family Barber Bait and Tackle had a real rowboat hanging in the window filled with fishing hats.

"I guess ninety-four hats," Elin said.

"Seventy-three," Andrew said. They guessed every time they passed, but they had never stopped to count the hats to see if either was right. Andrew always made her figure out the difference between their two guesses, though, for arithmetic practice.

"Twenty-one!"

"Correct."

They passed a drugstore, Crutch and MacDonald's, the police station, and the post office before stopping at the general store, which was attached to a small restaurant. In nearly every case, the general store had everything they needed: tools, paint, fabric, pots and pans, and food like flour, sugar, and butter. If it didn't, they had to go to Hopkinton, twenty miles inland. Elin had only visited Hopkinton twice, and both visits were short. The clock was always moving toward dusk, when they needed to be back on the island to light the lamp.

Andrew had made a deal with Stan Cooke, the owner of the General Store, that Stan could take half for every painting he sold. Stan liked Andrew, and he had space in one window, so he let Andrew put his paintings there.

"It might be a little late in the season to be bringing in more of these," Andrew said, thinking aloud. "I don't know why I didn't think of that earlier. Most of the summer folks have gone back to the city already."

"I'll bet most of them are staying through the weekend," Elin said. "The rentals usually run through Saturday."

Andrew nodded and brightened a little. "You're probably right, El. And maybe one of these newsmen will want to take a little piece of Maine back to Washington, D.C., or New York City, or wherever they're from."

There were lots of men milling about in front of Stan's store. Many were smoking cigarettes as they huddled in restless groups of three or four. Elin and Andrew threaded through the crowd to reach the entrance. Elin listened hard to pieces of conversations, trying to catch a clue to the mystery.

". . . how a summer day can start so much like a February one," one man was complaining to another.

". . . fog cleared out early. You arrive in that storm last night, too? Wind was so fierce it nearly blew my umbrella inside out!" she heard as she passed another group of men.

Elin held the door for Andrew, and he stepped in sideways to avoid damaging the paintings. He nearly collided with two small boys, who were rushing to get out with bags of penny candy. They pressed against him, and for a moment there was a stand-off.

"Whoa, hang on boys!" Andrew chuckled. "Just let me get in, and then you can get out."

The littlest one stepped back, shoving the other backward as he did.

"Licorice pieces, ten for a penny, today only," the little one said in explanation. His friend nodded and held up the bag as proof.

"Aren't you lucky!" Andrew said. He continued to move through the doorway, glancing at each side to be sure nothing was hitting. Elin followed, keeping the door from slamming against him. Once they were safely inside, the boys whooped out the door with their booty toward bikes lying in a heap by the step. Elin watched as they untangled the handlebars and then jumped on and wobbled down the road, candy bags bouncing with every rut and bump. For an instant, she envied their freedom.

Andrew walked toward his window display. He set the paintings down, then checked the pieces that were already set up.

"Look at this, El," he said. "Stan sold all of the gull paintings and two of the ones of that old rowboat that washed up on shore. He even sold the one I did of the house! I wasn't too fond of that one, actually."

Elin didn't answer. She was looking about the store. Usually they had it to themselves. But today, men—strangers all—were strolling the aisles in trench coats, poking with impatience through the candy on the rack, reading the magazine covers with their hands pushed into deep pockets. She glanced around to see if Dan might be there, but then caught herself, annoyed. Dan was probably home by now, trying to explain the sunken boat to his parents. Why was he on her mind at all? She vigorously shook her head, as if by doing so she could force away such silly images.

Andrew stood with his hand raised for a few minutes, trying to get Stan's attention. But Stan was hustling about behind the counter, finding pipe tobacco for one customer, taking a dime for a bottle of soda from another. Finally Andrew said, "Let's just set them up. I'll let him know what we've done on the way out."

Elin had her back to her father. "Can I ask one of the men what's going on?"

Andrew glanced around the store. "You can ask," he said finally. "But I'll need you to stand outside and tell me how these look, so be quick."

"I'll be back in a flash," Elin promised.

She followed the aisle to the end where a man stood

with a notebook tucked under his arm. He was reading the weekly Rock Point paper and chuckling.

She hesitated, waiting for her courage to build.

"Excuse me," she said.

He finished reading, then snickered again, and dropped the paper back in the pile. He stared at Elin. "You want me, young lady?"

"Well, yes," Elin began. Suddenly the words did not come easily. "I was just noticing the people . . . lots of people outside . . . and wondering just what everyone is, well, is doing here." There. She looked up at him with an expectant smile.

He stared back, as if trying to decide whether or not she was worth his time. "You live here?"

Elin nodded. "On Oyster Island." She made a vague motion toward the shore.

"On an island, no fooling?" He cocked his head and, as if by instinct, released the notebook from against his side, grasped it, and flipped it open. "You live out there year-round, do you?"

"Yes. My father is the lightkeeper. So, uh, why are so many newsmen here today?"

"A lighthouse family. Interesting." He regarded her for a few long minutes. Then he scribbled something in his book. Elin began to wonder if he had any intention of answering her question.

"Did a boat capsize or something?" she asked in a small voice.

The man let out a short laugh. "How old are you, lighthouse girl?"

"Thirteen."

"Well, then, you know who the president of the United States is, don't you?"

"Of course. Franklin Roosevelt. My father named our bird after him."

"Bird?" The man frowned at her. But his expression softened as she continued to look at him attentively. "Roosevelt. That's right. Well, would you like to see him?"

See the president? Was he teasing? "Well, I certainly would," she said after a thoughtful pause. "But how would I be able to do that?"

"Just wait around here for a while," the man said. "That's what we're all doing. He's coming back from a meeting with Churchill. They had to talk about how to beat the Nazis." He looked at her through narrowed eyes. "You know who Churchill is?"

"The prime minister of Great Britain."

"Good." He seemed pleased that he was not wasting his time on an uninformed audience.

"Well, it was a very important meeting. Top secret location. Somewhere in the North Atlantic. Probably Newfoundland. And unfortunately—" the man began leafing through his worn notebook, the pages covered on both sides with pencil scratches— "we had to hear about it from the Brits. They were reporting on what was being said before we knew there was any talking going on. I still can't believe that we weren't notified once the talks were under way—" He looked up, as if suddenly aware that he wasn't talking to a fellow reporter.

"Well, at any rate, young lady," he concluded, snapping his notebook closed and turning toward the door, "your president and mine is on his way here any time now. And that's what all the fuss is about." Elin could hear him muttering as he walked out.

"Lighthouse family. Could be a story in that, especially with the war." He jerked the door closed behind him.

Chapter 4

THE PRESIDENT! COMING here! To Rock Point!

Elin spun about, looking for Andrew. He was still across the store in the window, setting up his pictures on the easels. "Andrew! You'll never believe it!" she shouted as she ran to him.

He finished straightening the fish picture, then stood up and crossed his arms. "Now, what will I never believe?" he asked.

"The president is coming here! President Roosevelt! That's why all these reporters are here!"

Andrew looked at her. His face showed no reaction.

"Aren't you excited, Andrew?"

"Why is he coming here?"

"But aren't you excited?" Elin persisted.

"Depends on why he's coming," Andrew said.

"Oh, he had a meeting with Churchill somewhere out in the middle of the ocean—a *secret* meeting," Elin said. "About the . . . Nazis, I think. Anyway, can we stay and wait for him? I want to meet him!"

Andrew stared over her head. Then he sighed and returned to his paintings. "If he comes while we're here, we'll see him," he said. "But we can't wait around. I have a lot of chores to do before sundown."

"Chores," Elin grumbled. "Chores, chores, chores. Who cares about chores when the president of the entire country is coming right here?" She knew she sounded like a spoiled five-year-old, but at that moment she didn't care.

Andrew did not look at her as he fiddled with the legs of an easel to make it stand upright. He sat back to check it out. He fussed some more, and then stood up. "Elin, go outside and see what this looks like."

Elin heaved a dramatic sigh and plodded toward the door. She yanked it open and shuffled over to the window. Glaring at Andrew through the glass, she folded her arms in front of her. He held his hands palms up as if to ask her, 'So, how do they look?' She shrugged in response and pointed to the piece of cardboard with his name on it. It had slipped under one of the easels. He smiled and nodded, reaching over to pick it up. She clomped back inside. Andrew ignored her attitude.

"I need to stop at Henry's and grab some hooks," he said. "Then we'll come back for a bite to eat."

On their way out, Andrew managed to catch Stan's eye and pointed toward the window. Stan replied with a sloppy salute.

The general store was near the Family Barber Bait and Tackle. One of the reporters was talking to Henry Appy, the owner, in the doorway, while another man set up a camera to take a picture of the front window and sign. From the questions the reporter was asking, it sounded as though he thought it was quite funny that a store that sold haircuts would also sell fish bait.

He has no idea what people who live here need from a store, she thought. Whenever Andrew went in for a haircut, he came out with fishing line or a piece of netting to repair a lobster trap. And sometimes when he went in for fishing supplies, he came out with a trim, because he usually needed one. And Mr. Appy was always chatting about the latest news, and Andrew wanted to hear it.

"I'll wait outside," Elin said, still pouting.

"Elin," Andrew said, putting his hands on her shoulders and turning her toward him. "Don't you think I know how thrilling it would be to see the president? Don't you think I want you to be able to do that? But you and I both know that we have a commitment on the island that is more important than anything else, even seeing the president of the United States in our own town. Right? And what would Sarah think if we didn't return on time? She'd be terribly worried, and we don't want to stress her heart, remember?"

Elin looked at the ground. She knew about Sarah's weak heart. And she knew that the lantern had to be lit one half-hour before sundown. How often had she heard that? She knew it as well as she knew her name. Of course there could be no exceptions. Of course Andrew was right. Only right now she didn't feel like being reasonable. She just wanted to be cross.

She nodded once, and Andrew accepted it as proper acknowledgement.

"I'll be right out," he said.

The midday sun was strong. The breeze that was such a part of her life on the island was weak here. Feeling too warm, Elin wriggled out of her sweater and tied it around her waist. She watched as the photographer clicked several shots of the big storefront window, crowded with signs telling how much everything cost—a shave or a haircut or a bucket of eels.

She wondered if the photograph would show the rowboat full of hats on the other side of the glass. It took him so long to adjust the different parts of the camera to his liking that Elin couldn't imagine what he would do with a subject that moved, like a train or a horse. He certainly couldn't take such a long time for each picture. When he eventually leaned over to hoist the camera and tripod onto his shoulder, Elin ambled over and sat on the narrow window sill.

She surveyed the scene from her perch, feeling wonderfully invisible against the distracting collage in the window. She watched the newsmen pacing back and forth, many smoking cigars or cigarettes, their dark hats shading their eyes. They gathered in groups of two or three, but never seemed to stop moving.

A group of four teenage girls turned onto Main Street, walking toward her. They leaned into one another so that their heads were nearly touching. They seemed to be discussing something of great importance. Maybe they wanted to meet the president, too. Elin marveled that they could walk, leaning like that. Maybe they were holding each other up.

As they approached her, she noticed that the girls were dressed alike, with light-colored blouses and skirts that ended just at the knee, and black-and-white shoes. Elin stared down. Every girl wore mismatched socks. They were giggling as they passed by, and Elin heard one of them mention something about a Jailbird Dance.

She continued to gaze at them as they moved by, admiring their identical hair, pulled back neatly from their faces with smooth curls bouncing on their shoulders as they walked. She reached up to stroke her braids. Sarah had wanted to redo them this morning, but Elin had refused, insisting that they looked fine. But now she was aware of stray hairs poking out of the plaits at random, the result of a restless night's sleep.

Her hands moved from her braids, down the simple shirt that Sarah had made, to her dungarees, nearly worn through at the knees. With her brown boots completing the picture, she knew she looked more like a fisherman than a teenage girl.

The door of the barber and bait shop opened and Andrew stepped out with a bag and some folded newspapers under his arm. He motioned to her.

"I'll be there in a second," she said. He nodded and strode back to the general store.

Elin stayed outside for a few minutes longer, waiting to see if the girls would return, but they didn't. She finally wandered into the store and walked to the back, where there was a narrow hallway with a row of bakery shelves along one side. The shelves were crammed with neat rows of little cakes and muffins, pastries and cookies. On the other side of the hallway, behind the display counter, several women in white caps and white aprons kneaded bread dough, dripped icing on cinnamon buns, or tossed cooled loaves of bread into paper sacks, twirling the ends to make them stay closed. Elin inhaled deeply, taking in the warm, moist smell of things baking.

One of the women turned when she heard footsteps. Her wide face was dusted with flour and Elin couldn't help smiling.

"Hello, Elin," she said. "How about taking some goodies back to the island with you?" She patted her floury hands on her apron, sending up a cloud of white. "Are you going to bring your mother some of my cinnamon buns? She loves them so, and she can't make them herself. She told me she's tried!"

Elin knew that, having eaten many a cinnamon bun that hadn't quite met with Sarah's satisfaction. "Sure," she said. "I'll remind Andrew to pick some up before we go back."

The floured lady nodded, satisfied, and turned back to her kneading.

Elin walked down the hall that opened into a small restaurant with a few tables scattered about and a row of stools along a counter. The tables were usually empty and the counter full. Today, though, some of the newsmen were lounging at the tables, hats off and smoking cigarettes or studying their notebooks.

As Elin stepped into the restaurant, she stopped to talk to Rosie. Rosie was a brightly colored parrot with lots of things to say.

"Hello, Rosie," she said. "How's Rosie today?"

"Hello, hello," the bird replied. "Hello, hello! Eat here, will you? Hello!"

Elin giggled and looked around for Andrew. He was sitting on a stool with his back to her. His long legs were bent so that his feet could grab the footrest under the counter. Between his legs rested his large package from the tackle shop. He was hunched over his coffee cup, talking to an old fisherman and a Coast Guard officer sitting next to him. More accurately, they were talking and he was listening. Andrew was stirring his coffee but not drinking it. Just stirring, stirring.

Elin climbed onto the empty stool next to him. She tried to get Millie's attention to order, but the waitress was bustling about behind the counter in a dither, clutching a handful of order slips, muttering. She rushed over to Eddie, the cook, and began dictating in a loud voice. "Two cheeseburgers, a ham sandwich on light toast, butter on the toast . . ."

Elin gazed up at the chalkboard that gave the day's

menu. She really didn't have to look—it never changed. In fact, she didn't think that anyone had ever changed the writing on the chalkboard since she could first remember reading it. The words were faded now, and there were places where something had rubbed up against the board and wiped off some of the letters. But she knew what it said, and she always ordered a grilled cheese sandwich and chocolate milk for 35 cents. Chocolate milk was one thing she never had at home.

Thinking about milk made her even thirstier, and she waved at Millie. But Millie didn't see her, or pretended not to, and continued bouncing about, filling a coffee cup here, sliding a plate filled with meatloaf and potatoes over there. Elin heaved an annoyed sigh, and rested her chin in her hands. She tipped her head toward Andrew to hear what the men were talking about but kept her eyes focused on Millie, waiting for her chance.

"This is getting mighty serious," someone near Andrew was saying. "We're about as much at war as we can be without actually firing bullets."

"Mmmmm," another deep voice agreed. "Something's going to happen soon, it does seem. This secret meeting with Churchill, well, it's likely to mean that our time is coming. How much longer can we stay out of things, after all?"

"What's going to happen out on the island, Whitcomb?" the first voice asked. "I heard that a good number of lighthouse beams on the East Coast—hundreds—will have to be darkened. Dimmed at the very least."

Elin took her eyes off Millie and leaned forward. It was the old fisherman who had just spoken. She recognized him, although she couldn't remember his name. She didn't know the Coast Guard officer who sat with them. Looking from one to the other, she couldn't imagine a sharper contrast: the young officer in his crisp, white uniform with pleats where they were supposed to be and none where they weren't, and the old fisherman, unshaven and untucked, with clothes as worn and weathered as his face. She waited for someone to explain about the lighthouse.

Andrew stopped stirring. "Certainly the war has not come to Maine, has it?" he asked. Elin heard an uneasy smile in his voice.

The Coast Guard officer cleared his throat. "Well, it has come to the East Coast," he said. "German U-boats were spotted not long ago near Cape Henry."

"Is that right?" Elin could hear the surprise in Andrew's voice.

"It seems that the British have gotten quite good at detecting U-boats with radar," the Coast Guard officer said, "and attacking them from the air. My guess is—"

"Those Germans," the old man interrupted, "have their sights set on our coast next, I'd betcha anything, now that we've been pulled into the fray. They're aiming to interrupt our shipping routes."

"Could be," the officer agreed. He took a long sip of his coffee. "In any case, the war's reached our shore, I'm afraid. Or at least it's heading our way mighty quick. From what you say, Andrew, your island is pretty remote. No one would be able to reach you in the event of an air raid."

An air raid? Elin thought. What's that?

"You could rent something near town until, well, until whenever," the old man offered. "Move the family off the island for awhile and—"

"But we need to keep the light going," Elin interrupted. "Our light keeps boats from hitting the reefs. Don't you know that?"

The three men turned to look at her.

"Oh, Elin," Andrew said. "I didn't realize you were sitting there. Mind your manners. Don't interrupt grownups." He twisted the stool back toward the men. "My daughter, Elin."

Both men nodded.

"People need our light," Elin repeated. "It helps people."

The officer looked at Andrew as if seeking his help in answering. Andrew was silent.

"I'm afraid that these days it helps the wrong people," the officer said finally.

"What?" Elin said. "I don't understand."

"It shows the Germans where to lay mines," he explained, "and the beam silhouettes ships at night, making them easy targets for subs. So it's more of an aid to the enemy these days than a friendly warning to sailors." He tipped his head back and gulped down the last of his coffee.

As he slid off the chair and reached into his pocket for change, he added, "It's a different world today than last week. And different last week from last year. Every day, we're moving closer to being a world at war."

He plunked some dimes next to his cup and slid his white hat off the counter. "Good luck," he said to Andrew and strode out of the restaurant.

Elin watched him go with a frown. Andrew stood and reached for money, too. His coffee cup was nearly full. "Elin, you never got anything to eat. Are you hungry?"

Elin shook her head.

The old man fished in his front pocket.

"I've got it, Wally," Andrew said. He slid the coins toward the back of the counter.

"Why, thanks, Whitcomb." Wally took a few minutes to lift himself off the stool.

"Young lady," he said to Elin once he'd straightened and hitched up his pants, "just think. No matter what happens, you'll be able to tell your grandchildren about growing up on an island, daughter of a lighthouse keeper. Won't that make for some interesting stories!"

Elin didn't respond. She was thinking about what the officer had said. About subs and torpedoes. About a whole world at war. Her head was full of thoughts of faraway troubles, in countries she knew only from the pages of newspapers, over problems she didn't understand.

But for some reason she remembered the cinnamon buns. "Andrew, may I have money to buy some cinnamon buns for Sarah?"

"Why, sure," he said. He felt in his pocket and found a quarter. "Whatever this will buy."

"Thanks, Andrew."

Elin walked back to the bakery counter. There was a woman in front of her buying some bread, so Elin stood staring through the glass at the baked goods. A world war. Her eyes were fixed on the blueberry muffins, but her mind was at sea, chasing German subs, and in the air, watching airplanes dropping bombs and then veering away after confirming a hit. Soldiers, tanks, fox holes, all the things she'd read about and tried to imagine. All of it was moving closer.

"Hello!" The floured lady behind the counter was calling to Elin. "Can I help you, dear?"

"Oh, I'm sorry." Elin returned to the bakery. "Uh, a quarter's worth of cinnamon buns, please."

The lady looked pleased as she tossed a half dozen into a paper bag. "Oh, it's a hard recipe to copy, that's for sure," she beamed. "So many ladies try to make these at home, and they just can't get it quite right. Just like my tarts. No one can seem to make those the same, either. Like some of them, too?"

"Oh, no thank you," Elin said. Why was this lady talking about her tarts when there was a war going on?

She handed the bag to Elin in exchange for the quarter. "You give my best to your mother, now."

"Of course." Elin folded down the top of the bag and went back for Andrew.

His stool was empty, but Millie had found a free moment. Her mouth was puckered around a soda straw.

"Excuse me," Elin said. "Do you know where Andrew Whitcomb has gone?"

"I believe I heard him say he was headed for the post office and then for home."

"Thank you." Elin walked to the restaurant door, then changed her mind. She made her way back through the restaurant, down the bakery hallway, and back to the general store.

She went over to the window where Andrew's paintings were on display. The lighthouse, sunset, waves . . . where was the one of her?

"Mr. Stan," she called across the store. "Did you already sell one of Andrew's paintings?"

Stan turned a weary face from his cash register. A newsman was just leaving with pipe tobacco and a copy of the paper.

"Dearie, it's been so busy in here this morning, I don't know what I've sold or to whom. I might've sold one of the paintings. I don't even have this kind of crowd on the week before the Fourth of July, you know! And everyone in such a hurry! Rush, rush, rush! You'd think five minutes one way or the other would actually make a difference."

He turned to the next man in line. "What do you need, young man?"

Elin looked once more from one painting to the next. They were all there, except for the one of her and the lighthouse. She turned away and walked slowly back to the wharf, poking at the unspent coins in her pocket.

Andrew had untied the ropes and tossed them into the boat. He was ready to go, his package from the bait store already neatly tucked under the stern seat. "Sarah will be happy you bought these cinnamon buns," he said.

Elin barely heard him. Her ears were still filled with the words from the restaurant. She stepped in and took her seat in the front. Andrew jumped in, gave a shove, and jerked on the cord to start the motor. The boat jumped away from the wharf.

Elin watched as the docks slipped away, and the seaside mansions became dollhouses. The deep green hills of late summer fell back until the trees were no more than splotches of green. With every sputter of the motor, every section of wake, they were farther from the chaos, the crowds, the strange faces of newsmen and their cameras and notebooks. They left behind the Coast Guard officer, Wally the old fisherman, and their talk of the war.

She and Andrew rode out to the island without speaking, the boat slicing into the waves like a sharp knife. Elin let her hand hang over the side of the boat. As the sea licked her fingers, she thought about the fish these waters had given them for so many suppers, like the seven-pound codfish she had caught just a few weeks ago. When Sarah cut it open in the kitchen, she found a solid gold ring inside with the initial "E" on it. Elin felt around her neck. It was still there, hanging from a length of fishing line.

Would Andrew take her fishing if they were living on the mainland and able to walk to the store for groceries? She shook her head vigorously to get rid of such thoughts.

She shifted into the middle seat where she could face forward and see the familiar whale shape of the island with the lighthouse as its spout and the scrub pine forest growing out of its tail.

As the boat headed for the island like a homing pigeon, Elin saw Sarah on the dock, waving. Gulls circled around her, dipping and swooping. She must have just finished cleaning fish for the chowder. The birds were waiting for her to head back to the house so they could finish off what was left. Andrew cut the motor and pulled out the paddle. Sarah strolled to the end of the dock, her bucket of fish on one arm, the other outstretched to catch the end of the paddle.

"Welcome back," Sarah sang out.

They were home. It didn't matter what those men had said, Elin thought. Her world wasn't at war.

"I don't want to tell my grandchildren," she said to Andrew as she grabbed the dock. "I want them to see everything for themselves."

Andrew stared down at the waves that rolled under the pier and splashed onto the rocky shore. He patted Elin's arm without seeming to notice. "That may not be possible," he said into the sea.

Chapter 5

AS ONE PEACEFUL day on the island blended seamlessly into the next, and the next, Elin found it easier not to dwell on the disturbing news she'd overheard at the diner. With renewed enthusiasm, she embraced the familiar routine: washing on Monday, baking on Tuesday, mending and ironing on Wednesday, dusting on Thursday, gathering and stacking wood on Friday, helping Andrew paint or polish on Saturday. And of course there was schoolwork and chores like sweeping and cooking that needed to be done every day. Her mind comfortably occupied, Elin's trip to Rock Point faded to an unpleasant, distant memory.

Even when Andrew read aloud from the newspapers he'd brought back about test blackouts or about Germany invading Poland or Italy declaring war on France, she could force herself to stay calm. She knew that after Andrew had finished reading, he would ask her questions to see what she remembered as Sarah leafed through the pages and clipped recipes. Then the papers would be stacked up near the kindling wood in the kitchen and fed one by one to the fire, exploding into flames and crumbling into a heap of ashes. With the words gone, it was as if the faraway war vanished completely.

Andrew didn't return to the mainland for three weeks. This time, Elin chose to stay at home and help Sarah. She did not want to go and, besides, Sarah had not been feeling well for several days and on this morning she looked particularly tired.

Andrew left early with the promise that he would be back well before noon. He just needed to pick up the mail and some groceries. Elin watched from the dock as the little boat hopped over the swollen waves toward town. When the boat was so far away that it didn't even look as if it were moving, she turned and walked back to the house.

Sarah was already bent over the tub, scrubbing an old pair of Andrew's pants against the washboard.

"Do you smell the rain?" she asked as Elin walked into the kitchen.

"Hmmm, now that you mention it, I guess I do." Elin grabbed the sack of dirty clothes and reached in for one of Sarah's dresses. "Let me do that, Sarah," she insisted.

But Sarah waved her off. "You empty the ashes and sweep up by the stove," she said. "Then you can dust in your room and ours. By the time you've done that, everything will be ready to hang out. Let's hope the rain holds out until they're dry."

It took Elin the rest of the morning to finish her chores and join Sarah outside. With the hazy sun hanging directly overhead, she helped Sarah finish pinning up the sheets and pillowcases. They billowed out, dancing tirelessly with the ocean breeze, tugging at the clothespins that gripped them.

Elin stepped toward them, then dashed away as they lunged at her. "They're trying to lick me!" she shrieked. She waited for Sarah to scold her for acting so silly when there was work to be done. Or to remind her that the Inspector insisted that the wash be off the lines by one o'clock. But Sarah didn't say anything. So Elin ducked and dove to avoid the huge, wet, white tongues until she saw that Sarah had dragged over another basket of wash. She scurried away from the playful sheets and grabbed a damp towel from the top.

Sarah's long braid, a weaving of brown and gray, brushed the ground as she knelt to pick up the bag of clothespins. Elin held out her hand for the two she needed. But Sarah didn't give them to her, and she didn't stand back up. Hunched over, she staggered backward and sank to the ground.

"Sarah, what's the matter?" Elin knelt over her. When Sarah looked up, her gray eyes were like frantic storm clouds and her face was the color of the sheets. Elin yanked a nearly dry towel off the line and hastily spread it out on the ground behind her. "Lie down," she ordered. "I'll . . . I'll get help."

She charged down the grassy slope toward the pitch pines, praying that when she reached the beach, Andrew's boat would be in sight. The only other boat on the island was a haggard old rowboat with a mismatched set of oars. She couldn't imagine rowing ten ocean miles in that vessel under any circumstances, never mind with Sarah so sick beside her.

As she leaped through the pine forest like a deer, her mind was moving even faster than her legs, scrolling quickly through her limited options. She had no telephone, no two-way radio, no way to call for help. There was the foghorn. If she blew the fog siren and if Andrew heard it, he would know that something was wrong. But it would take the better part of an hour to get it up and running. And how long would it take for Andrew to get back to the island once he realized there was a problem?

Elin charged onto the beach and rounded the corner of the island, scanning the waves for the boat. She began to panic as the uninterrupted water view revealed nothing. Then, as she raced along the beach that wrapped around the island's western side, she saw a far-off spot. She ran to the very end of the wharf, drawing in deep and anxious breaths. She strained to see details on the smudge. It had to be Andrew's boat. At the very least, she prayed, please let it be someone headed for their island.

The spot seemed to be frozen on the water.

Come on! she pleaded silently. Come *here*.

She strained so hard to see that the shape blurred, then grew, then shrunk, then disappeared altogether. She scrunched her eyes up to force them to rest, then looked out at the water again. This time, the spot seemed larger.

Her thoughts raced back to Sarah. Was she awake? Or was she unaware of everything? Elin fought the idea of running back to her with the news that she'd spotted a boat. No use getting Sarah's hopes up if the faraway boat moved away, blissfully unaware of the tragedy that was descending on their island.

Elin hopped up and down, shaking the dock on its wave-weakened piers, releasing the energy that wanted to burst out of her. The boat was getting bigger. It surely was. And it seemed to be heading for the island. Soon she would know whether or not it was Andrew.

Five minutes stretched into ten as Elin stared the boat down, trying to draw it to the island through the power of her wishes. It had to be nearly fifteen minutes now from when she had left Sarah's side, and she knew for sure. The boat was heading for the island, and it was Andrew's boat.

She leapt off the dock, exhausted with gratitude and relief, and ran back to Sarah. She lay just as Elin had left her, on the towel near the clothesline, eyes closed, hands resting tensely on her chest.

"Sarah, he's here! Andrew's back!" It was hard to keep the tremble out of her voice. "I'm going to go back and bring him right here, all right? I won't be gone long."

Elin was calling out to Andrew long before he could hear her. The story spilled out as his boat droned closer. When he finally cut the motor, she shouted the news again. As Andrew closed the gap with the dock, he tossed a bag full of papers and packages onto the dry boards and hopped out. Flipping the rope to Elin, he asked, "Where is she?"

"Side yard," Elin told him as she quickly secured the boat. Neither spoke as they raced back up the hill toward the house.

Andrew dropped beside Sarah and put his face close to hers. After he spoke quietly to her for a few minutes, she murmured in his ear without opening her eyes. He squeezed her hand and turned to Elin. "Blanket, please?"

Elin nodded and dashed off to her parents' bedroom, wanting so badly to ask what was wrong but knowing that it was not the right time.

She returned quickly. Andrew wrapped the blanket tightly around Sarah. He lifted her up and carried her like a baby to the beach. Elin hurried along behind him. He rested for just a moment at the water's edge, then strode down the strip of sand to the wharf. Gently, he settled Sarah on the boat's middle seat and turned to Elin.

"You're going to have to take care of things on your own for a day or two, maybe more." His voice sounded graver than she had ever heard it. "You know as much about the light as I do, and you can certainly take care of Sarah's duties. I'll be back as soon as I can."

"What's wrong with her, Andrew?" Elin stared with alarm at the silent bundle in the boat. Sarah's eyes were still closed and she was slumped forward.

"I don't know. Likely it's her heart. We'll go straight to Doc Simington's office when we get to Rock Point. He'll be able to take care of her, I'm sure." But he didn't look sure.

"But can't I come?" Elin heard the whine in her own voice, but she didn't care. "I want to know what's wrong with her. I want to be there with you. Isn't there a full moon tonight? No one will miss the light. And remember what that Coast Guard officer said about the light doing more harm than good? Pleeease?" As she pleaded, she felt ashamed. But the thought of being apart from Sarah right now, and being in charge of the light . . .

"This light has shone every night for a hundred and twenty-two years, Elin." That was all he said as he forced the boat away from the dock. He thrust the oars deep into the waves and pulled back. Soon he had worked the boat away from the dock. As he leaned over to yank the rope that started the motor, he turned toward Elin. "I'll send—" but his voice was drowned out by the surf.

"What, Andrew?" Elin hollered back.

But now the motor was roaring and the boat lurched toward the far-off black line that was Rock Point. Elin watched as the boat grew smaller and the drone of the motor mingled with the restless ocean.

"Andrew!" she shouted, her hands cupped around her mouth. "Saaa-raaah! Don't leave me here!" The ocean gusts tossed her words back to her, sounding like an ungrateful child. Always, before, there had been someone nearby to answer.

Elin wanted to be worrying only about Sarah, who looked so sick, but right this minute she couldn't because she was worrying too much about herself. Never in her thirteen years had she ever been left alone.

Against her will, tears filled her eyes and then spilled down her cheeks.

Chapter 6

BANG! ELIN LET the back screen door slam shut. It was nice to hear a familiar noise. She shoved the inner door closed with her boot. Franklin made a lazy turn toward the window with the chilly gust that followed her in.

"Hello, Franklin," Elin said. Her words sounded too loud, and seemed to hang in the air, having disrupted the stillness. Not that the place wasn't quiet when Sarah and Andrew were sleeping or reading in the living room, but this was a different kind of quiet. A lonesome, empty kind of quiet.

"Do you miss Sarah, Franklin? She's not humming to you while she does the dishes, is she?" He twirled slowly in response and found a resting spot.

In the dishpan, a few cups still bobbed in the now cool gray water. She dropped Andrew's packages on the table and moved to the sink to wash and rinse the cups and set them on the rack to dry. As she wandered outside to hang up the damp dish cloth, she noticed that the towels she had dropped when Sarah collapsed were still lying on the ground in a heap, a disturbing tribute to that moment in time. She shook them out and hung them up along with the rest of the damp clothes in the basket. She was not going to worry about the Inspector and his unbending rules today. Even though the sheets still urged her to dance with them, she didn't feel like it.

She plopped onto the back stoop, thinking about what to do next. She wondered if, from the tower, she would still be able to see their boat. But there was no need to go up. Andrew had already taken care of the light for the day, so there was nothing to be done until one half hour before sunset when the lamp needed to be lit.

What would Sarah be telling her to do now? Mop the kitchen floor, probably, and add coal to the stove. Check to see if any of the vegetables in her buckets needed to be picked; there were a few tomatoes still struggling to ripen in the chilly autumn air. Collect wood, of course, and fill the lamps with kerosene, work on the sweater she was knitting. The dog needed to be fed, and so did the chickens. The eggs should be collected. Elin sighed. She forced herself up and trudged toward the coop.

It was late afternoon when Elin stood the mop in the corner of the kitchen. She pictured Sarah standing by the sink. She would turn and say, "Elin! What a tremendous help you've been! You've done your own chores and mine as well! Look at the neat beds you made! And, my, there's not a speck of dirt on the floor. What would I ever do without you?" She would have said that had she been there.

Elin perched on a chair. The kitchen looked so different without Sarah in it, or at least without the possibility that she would be walking in at any minute. And it smelled different. It had a vacant, nobody's-home kind of smell. No fish chowder was bubbling away on the stove, no apple pie scent drifted across the room.

Elin's stomach told her that it would be time for dinner soon. She'd forgotten lunch in the chaos. Through the window over the table she saw the sun creeping toward the distant Maine coastline. She wondered if Sarah and Andrew were watching the sun right now, too, or if they were thinking about her.

In the cool cupboard she found leftover baked beans from Saturday night's supper. She knew she should open some jars of green beans or corn, but she didn't.

"I am going to have a dinner made up of very few vegetables and a great deal of dessert," she announced to the stove. Her voice sounded as loud as the foghorn. She added more coal to the tired lumps that were glowing a pale orange. As she shook down the ashes, she wondered why they hadn't gotten another coal delivery. She made a mental note to gather extra driftwood the next day. She could save the coal for nighttime and use the fast-burning wood during the day. When the stove began to radiate heat, she set the beans to warm in a pot on the stove and put out her lonely plate and cup.

She had never seen the table set for just one person before. She moved her plate around to see where she could put it to make it take up the most room. Then she moved the vase of dried flowers from the window sill over the sink to make the table seem fuller.

When the beans were sufficiently warm, she scooped them into a bowl and painted a buttermilk biscuit with strawberry jam. She poured herself a glass—extra tall—of Andrew's homemade root beer. Ignoring her napkin, she wiped a blob of jelly on her dungarees. Then she put her elbows on the table, just to see what it would feel like, because normally she wasn't allowed to. But now there was no one here to tell her what to do and what not to do. No one was handing her a napkin, or asking her if her dinner tasted good. No one was wondering if she wanted more root beer. No one cared that she was not eating any vegetables.

She stopped after a few bites to call Sailor. "Here, boy!" she shouted from the back door. "C'mere doggie!" He romped over from where he had been bothering the chickens, eager for dinner scraps. Elin held the door open wide.

"C'mon in, boy," she coaxed. He whimpered, then stepped back.

"I'm in charge, Sailor, and I say, 'Come!'"

Elin pulled him inside by the collar, his stubborn legs stiff, his nails scraping in protest against the kitchen floor. As soon as she'd dragged him all the way inside, she latched the door behind him.

"Come over here, boy," she demanded, sitting back down at the table. "Sit here, Sailor." But Sailor glanced around warily, then moped over to the door. Head low, he whined to be let out.

"Sailor, you're more 'fraidy-cat than dog." Elin let him out and took down the kerosene lamp from its hook. With care, she lit it and set it on the table near Andrew's pile of newspapers. The dark print demanded to be read in the bright light of the lamp. Elin glanced at the headlines as she scraped the last of the jelly from the plate with a chunk of her biscuit.

"Nazis Encircle Leningrad; Hitler plans to starve city to death"

"Jews in Germany Must Wear Star of David"

"Unidentified Sub Fires on U.S. Ship"

She turned the pages quickly, looking for the comics. She loved L'il Abner—Schmoo always made her laugh. She paused for just a few seconds on an article with pictures showing the latest fashions in women's hats and winter coats before continuing to leaf through the pages.

Suddenly a headline caught her attention: "Liberty's Torch Darkened for Duration of War." She hesitated, letting her gaze move across the words under the bold print. "Even in silence, she reveals too much . . . a landmark for enemy aircraft . . . a dangerous ally for Germany . . ." Elin carefully tore out the article to show to Andrew. She slid it to the side, then brought it back and read it again.

Abruptly, angrily, she wadded it into a ball and carried it to the stove. Prying open the lid, she dropped it in and watched it blacken and curl and disappear. Gone.

She cut herself a generous piece of chocolate zucchini cake that she decided to eat with her fingers and sat back down at the table.

When she shoved the rest of the newspapers aside, she saw that underneath was the pile of mail Andrew had brought from town. Elin pulled out a large package from the bottom of the pile. They rarely got packages.

Andrew's name was printed neatly on the front above "Lightkeeper, Oyster Island." The return address stumped her for a moment, and then she knew. It was from Dan and Jack. She considered opening it, even though it was not addressed to her. Well, why not? After all, it was obviously the borrowed clothes and maybe a thank you note. Nothing personal or private.

While she was considering this, she turned the package over in her hands. If it is Andrew's clothes, she told herself, the sooner they are out of the package and hung up, the less likely it would be that they would need ironing. This last thought was just enough to convince her to open it.

She untied the twine that bound the package tightly

and added it to the twine ball in the drawer. Then she unwrapped the layers of brown paper and laid them on the pile of paper by the stove. Inside were Andrew's clothes, washed and neatly folded, and two envelopes. One was addressed to Andrew and the other to her.

She opened the one for her, noting with a frown that her name was misspelled. She smoothed out the notepaper and began to read:

Dear Ellen,

It was nice to have met you the other day, although I'm sure you can imagine that I wish it had been under different circumstances. I'm sorry that Jack and I ran off so fast when we got to Rock Point, but we—or should I say "I"—had quite a lot of explaining to do. My parents were delighted that we were both alive and well, but much less delighted to hear what happened to the sailboat. I'm mopping floors and washing dishes at the diner after school and on the weekends to try to repay my uncle. It will probably take me until I am an old man, but it is the least I can do.

I'm writing not only to thank you, but to tell you that I've invited a group of my school chums to go to Hopkinton for a movie in two weeks (my birthday!). "Citizen Kane" is playing at the Colonial Theater there and it is supposed to be quite good. Afterward, we may go to Doogan's for an ice cream soda. I would love to have you join me. I know that you do not have a telephone, but perhaps you can write to me at Larkspur Lane in Rock Point.

Sincerely,
Dan Brooks

Elin read the letter three times, hearing Dan's voice as clearly as if he were reading it to her himself. Dan wanted her to go with him to the movies! She gulped away her fear and read the letter again. " . . . in two weeks . . ." She looked at the date in the corner and realized that the two weeks had shrunk to not much more than one week.

Of course she couldn't go. Not only because of Sarah being sick and all, but just because . . . well, it was all too strange and uncomfortable. She had never been to a movie. Sarah had told her what it was like to sit in a darkened theater and watch an immense, moving picture, but Elin couldn't even imagine it. And sitting in the dark with a group of "chums" she didn't even know? Shaking her head to solidify her decision, she folded the letter and returned it to the envelope.

Of course, if she did refuse—which she must—would he ever write to her again? It didn't matter that it was Dan, she assured herself, it was just nice to get mail. She wondered what Andrew and Sarah would say when she told them about the letter. She wondered if Sarah would insist that she go. Because if Sarah insisted, then . . .

She stood up and looked out the window. One-half hour before sunset. If Andrew and Sarah were here right now, she thought, Andrew would pull the checkers board out of the trunk in the living room and set it up on the table. He'd offer to let her start with five more checkers and she'd refuse. Four? No, sir! Three? Well, two then. All right, she'd start two ahead just to quiet him down. So they'd play, best two out of three, and he'd let her win the last game.

But not tonight. She put her dishes in the sink and wiped the crumbs off the table. Barely any scraps for Sailor tonight.

She held the lantern before her as she made her way through the passageway and up the gently curving lighthouse stairs. When she reached the lantern room, she squeezed through the window that opened onto the gallery. Gripping the narrow railing and looking across the world, over the miles of restless ocean, Elin strained to see the tiny lights that dotted the dark line where Maine met the sea. Somewhere over there, she imagined that Sarah was lying in a hospital bed. The doctors were making her well. Andrew was sitting beside her holding her hand, maybe reading to her from a magazine or a book. If only she could know for sure that the story playing in her mind was the true one.

Turning away from the sea, Elin slipped back through the open window to tend to her duties. After pulling off the covering, she filled the lamp's tank and lit the wick. She expertly put her finger into the flame to flick off the burned end the way Andrew did.

Before descending the ladder, she looked one last time in the direction of the faraway shore. Had Andrew been watching from some lofty perch to see whether the light would go on? If he was worried about her, he might have been, because the light would let him know that she was all right. But Elin doubted that he had any worrying left in him after using it up on poor Sarah.

In the house, she extinguished the kitchen light and went upstairs in semidarkness to get ready for bed. As the wind picked up and the rain that Sarah had smelled that morning began beating a pattern upon the roof, Elin pulled on her pajamas and worked her way under the icy covers. She said a longer prayer than usual, hoping that God would take notice and give Sarah some extra attention.

As she fell into a restless sleep, she dreamed of sitting with Sarah and Andrew in an overly warm hospital room. Sarah seemed fine, and was talking to Elin about going to the movies. All at once, Elin found herself in a huge, dark space, crowded with noisy teenagers. She was wearing her oldest pair of overalls, the ones that she only wore to help Andrew paint around the house and tower. Her boots were spattered with paint, and her hair hung in limp, day-old braids.

Suddenly, the attention of everyone in the vast, dark place was focused on her.

"Why do your socks match?" asked a girl who looked just like one of the girls that Elin had watched walk by at Rock Point.

"What's wrong with your hair?" asked another, her indistinct face looming from the crowd.

"Are you wearing *boots*?"

"What do you mean you haven't been to the movies before? How old are you, anyway?"

Elin stood up and fought to free herself, searching for a slice of light that would indicate an exit, a way out. She pushed through the chaos of teenagers, and now there were men in hats and coats holding notebooks and asking her questions about living on an island. She stumbled to the light and pushed. Falling out on the street, she hurled herself toward the harbor. She ran and ran, feeling her lungs straining to give her enough air, but when she finally reached the wharf, there were no boats. There was no way to get home. She turned, panting, and the crowd from the theater had followed her and was yelling her name. There was no boat to take her home. There was no way home! Home . . . home . . .

She awoke with a start, still panting. It took her a few seconds to remember that she was on the island, in her house, in her bedroom. She dropped back onto the pillow and pulled in some deep breaths. First thing in the morning, she would write back to Dan. Even before she had breakfast. She would explain that with Sarah unwell, she could not leave.

With that plan firmly in her mind, she relaxed against the bed's warmth and soon felt drowsy enough to sleep again. The ocean hugged the island like a blanket, and she was tucked safely inside.

Chapter 7

THE GRAY LIGHT of a new day groped its way into Elin's bedroom. As she stirred and stretched, she was jarred awake by . . . nothing. There was no noise coming from the kitchen. No voices, no smell of coffee or a hot breakfast waiting. As she sat up in bed, she shivered more from the strangeness of it all than from the icy chill of the morning air.

It took her a few minutes to recall why everything felt so different. Then the memory of Sarah's illness descended on her with a crushing force. She let the heavy weight of worry push her back down. Andrew and Sarah surely knew more about the illness now, more than they had yesterday. She wished for some way that they could let her know what the doctors had told them. It was the not knowing anything at all that was the most frightening.

Forcing herself up, she pulled on chilly clothes and wandered downstairs, glancing into Andrew and Sarah's room as she passed by. Their untouched bed stared back. In the kitchen, she peered into the stove's woodbox. The coal had long since gone cold. She rattled the handle so that the ashes would fall through, then lit some crumpled paper, urging the kindling to catch as she'd watched Sarah do hundreds of times before. After several tries, the fire burned hot enough so that she could add a shovelful of coal. She reminded herself about dragging some wood up from the beach.

As the circle of warmth from the stove spread, Elin felt the grip on her stomach relax. She made herself some oatmeal and opened a can of milk to drink. Then she headed for the tower to extinguish the light and cover the lens. From the lantern room, she stared hard at the pattern of waves, trying to make out a smudge that could be Andrew's boat. Nothing but the uninterrupted ocean stretched out, reaching for the distant shore. She plodded down the stairs and back to the kitchen.

It was Tuesday. Tuesday was baking day. Two loaves of bread, one pie, one pound cake, a dozen biscuits. That's what Sarah would make if she were here. If only.

Elin mixed the bread dough and covered it with a warm, damp cloth. She set it near the stove to rise and went outside to take care of the chickens and shovel out the coop. Only five eggs today. As the days grew shorter, there would be fewer eggs. Back in the kitchen, she punched and kneaded the loaves and returned them to the warmth to rise a second time. Then she made a list of what needed to be done that day. A list, she reasoned, would make the day go by more quickly. Every time she did a chore, she would check it off her list.

Her idea worked. Four hours passed easily, and her morning chores were done. She had only stopped to dwell on Sarah a few times, then she had managed to force her thoughts back to her jobs. Check, check, check, check. She studied her list with a sense of accomplishment. After lunch, it was just six checks until dinnertime. And then, perhaps, Andrew and Sarah would be back.

After making herself a simple soup of rice and vegetables, Elin hiked toward the beach to collect the driftwood that had washed up on shore. This was a two-check job—one check for gathering, the other for stacking. Dragging the ramshackle cart behind her, she remembered asking Andrew to fix the stuck wheel the day before Sarah got sick. The day before Sarah got sick. And this was the day after Sarah got sick. A new marker in their lives.

She paused at the edge of the pine grove to feel the island breathing. The breeze darted among the tufts of tall grass, sending them weaving this way and that. Even the stubby pitch pines shuddered as they were buffeted by the gusts from the sea. Elin tugged again to get the cart rolling, heading for the spot where she had stopped collecting wood a few days earlier.

The cart was half full when Elin discovered a perfect pink shell hiding under a piece of soggy wood. She dug it out of the sand and rinsed it off. Not even a chip! It was a perfect top shell!

"Sarah!" she called gleefully. Her voice was swept out to sea on the salty breeze. She grimaced. In her excitement, she had forgotten. Well, she would add it to her seashell garden by the back door. Sarah would be pleased when she returned.

Elin tucked the shell into her pocket. After she finished loading the cart, she hauled it back up the hill to the shed behind the house. She stacked the wood carefully, making sure that Andrew could still get to his tools that hung from nails on the wall. The last armful she brought into the kitchen and loaded into the stove.

~ ~ ~

The apple pie that was nearly done filled the kitchen with a "Sarah's home" kind of smell. She took it gratefully into her nostrils, over and over, until she couldn't smell it anymore.

She pulled out the bubbling pie and set in on the pie rack to cool. Looking with quiet pride at her lightly browned loaves of bread, the cake, and the biscuits, she knew that Sarah would be proud of her.

After she swept up the dusting of flour on the floor, she gave herself permission to read a book. Andrew had made a sheet of math problems for her but she could do those tomorrow. In about two hours, she would ascend the lighthouse stairs and light the light. Then she would go to bed, then wake up, then do it all over again.

She searched for a book on the shelf in the living room that would not remind her of Sarah. She could not read *The Five Little Peppers* because that was Sarah's favorite. *Grimm's Fairy Tales* would do. Andrew was partial to those, and she didn't mind dwelling on Andrew. Thoughts of him were happy ones.

She curled up on the sofa under the afghan that Sarah had knitted and she had pieced together. When she put her face into the soft wool, she was eight years old again, laying out the squares in a pattern on the floor while Sarah watched.

She began to grow drowsy as she read about Rumpelstiltskin and the miller's daughter. Her head nodded toward her chest as her mind filled with moving pictures of straw being spun into glistening gold by a crooked little man. She was jolted awake as the book dropped with a thud to the floor.

The quick descent of darkness caught her by surprise. Bursting from her afghan cocoon, she bolted for the kerosene lamp and trotted through the passageway, then took the tower stairs two at a time. When she reached the lantern room, she lit the lamp and dropped back through the trapdoor without looking across the water, sparing herself another inevitable disappointment.

Back in the kitchen, she had just enough energy to cut herself a slice of bread for dinner. She didn't bother to coat it with jam but swallowed it plain, just so that her empty stomach wouldn't be grumbling at her all night.

She trudged up the stairs and thought for a moment about getting into bed in her clothes. But she let her clothes drop to the floor in a heap and managed to pull a nightgown over her head. Once she was in bed, sleep quickly overcame her.

Minutes and hours sped by in time-altering sleep. Somewhere, in a deep dream, Elin heard Sailor barking. She half-woke and heard it again, a barking noise from somewhere distant. Her sleepy mind explained it away. Maybe one of the chickens had gotten loose. Sailor was chasing a chicken, though it had never happened before. And in her dozing dream, Sailor ran around after a huge chicken that was bigger than Andrew as Elin watched, acting as if there was nothing strange about it at all. And in the dream, she heard a sudden thump—a bumping noise that didn't seem to come from the huge chicken or from Sailor or from Elin. Then a dull thud.

In her groggy state, Elin wondered if she heard a noise downstairs. She didn't want to have to think about it. She was too tired to be concerned. She rolled over and pulled the covers over her head. Just as she was about to step back into her dream, she heard a muffled noise that she knew came from the kitchen. At this she propped herself up on her elbow and listened. Nothing more. Just old creaky house noises.

But as she buried her head in her pillow once again, she heard another thud. She strained to listen this time, to make sense of the sounds. She heard the scraping of the kitchen door as it opened and the quiet click of the screen door as someone closed it to avoid letting it bang.

Andrew! Andrew was home!

She threw back the covers. As she bounded across the room, her head filled with things she needed to tell him. She flung open her bedroom door and ran for the stairs.

It wasn't until she was thundering down the stairs that it occurred to her that Sailor never barked at Andrew. He only barked at strangers, like the Inspector and the lady from the school department. That realization hit her like a punch in the stomach as she reached the bottom step. She froze. For there in the kitchen doorway, outlined in black, stood a broad figure.

Elin knew with a dreadful certainty that it was not Andrew.

Chapter 8

ELIN TURNED IN terror and started to stumble back up the stairs, but she was stopped by a familiar voice.

"Elin! It's me!"

"Who?" Elin tried to keep the fear from rattling her voice, but she couldn't.

"It's Dan!"

Elin sank to the steps. Struggling to draw in a breath, she leaned forward and covered her face with her hands. "For God's sake, Dan," she whispered. "You scared me almost to death."

Dan took careful steps toward her, arms outstretched to feel his way in the darkness. When Elin looked up, his shadowy figure loomed before her.

"I'm sorry," he said. "I . . . I didn't want to wake you up. I thought I could just quietly come in and sleep on the sofa and talk to you in the morning."

Elin shook her head, trying to absorb what was happening. "Why . . . what are you doing here?" she asked.

"Your father asked me to come and check on you."

Elin sprang up and lunged down the stairs toward him. Surprised, he took a step back.

"You talked to Andrew? Is Sarah all right? What happened to her? What are the doctors saying?"

"She's doing all right." He held his hands up in front of him as if to protect himself from her exuberance. "She's still in the hospital. Seems she had a mild heart attack."

"But she's doing all right?"

"She's doing fine, and Andrew is staying with her at the hospital. They're taking good care of her."

Elin felt herself smile uncontrollably. "I was so worried. I mean, I had no idea what was happening over there and no way of finding out."

She paused to let herself revel in the news. For the first time in two days, she felt her chest relax, allowing her to pull in a deep breath.

"She's doing fine," she repeated quietly, as if to reassure herself. "She is going to be fine."

"Yes, she is," Dan said gently.

She raised her head sharply to look at him. She felt a newfound courage propelled by fear. "You said that my father sent you?"

"Yes, that's right."

Elin hesitated, then pushed past him and marched to where the kerosene lantern hung in the kitchen. She lit it and returned to the living room, further emboldened by the light. Holding it up to his face, she declared, "My father didn't send you."

"Yes, well, indirectly he did, yes."

Elin continued to hold the light up to his face. "What does that mean?"

"Well . . ." Dan shifted his weight from one leg to the other. "It means that he wanted somebody to come out here to check on you . . ."

"Yes?"

"Well, he had asked your cousin Ted—"

"I knew it!" Elin said. "I knew he wouldn't send you! I mean, he, *we* barely know you!"

Dan opened his mouth, then shut it again, staring down. "Well, I, uh . . . I gave Ted five bucks to let me come out here instead of him."

"Why?" Elin cocked her head and frowned.

"Because, I . . . well, I figure I owe you." Dan looked up and squinted in the sharp light of the lantern. "I should help you after all you did for me."

"But Andrew and Sarah would not approve of you being out here, without them, I mean. It's not . . . I mean, they would be . . ." Elin groped for the words to explain why they should not be alone on the island.

Dan didn't say anything for a moment. "I . . . I guess I didn't think of that." He frowned at something beyond the globe of lantern light. "Well, maybe I should leave in the morning, then?" His statement ended more like a question, as if he hoped she would disagree.

"I think that, yes, you should." Elin pulled the lantern away from his face. "You can sleep in my parents' room for tonight." She pointed toward the bedroom.

Dan nodded slowly.

He didn't say anything, so Elin thrust the lantern toward him and asked, "Do you need—"

"The lantern. Yes, thanks, I could use it."

She gave it to him and walked to the stairs. "I really don't need any help out here." Elin wasn't sure why she was re-stating the point. "I can handle things on my own. I've been doing just fine. Just fine."

"Right, I'm sure that's true." Dan sounded disappointed.

"Well . . . well, good night."

"Same, yes. Good night," he said, heading for the assigned bedroom.

Elin walked back up the stairs, her heart still beating fiercely, trying to recover from the few moments when it had stopped from pure terror. She returned to her room and to her bed, lying down and pulling up the covers without noticing what she was doing. She hadn't meant to sound so ungrateful. It wasn't that she didn't appreciate Dan coming to help. He had taken her by surprise, that was all, and he had frightened her.

Now that she knew Sarah was going to be all right, other odd bits and pieces of worry were rushing in to fill the place that had been devoted to worrying about Sarah. She did not know what to do about Dan. What should she say to him in the morning? Maybe he would leave before she came downstairs. It wasn't that she didn't like it when he was around, it was that she didn't like *herself* when he was around. He made her feel too aware of everything she said and did.

She flipped onto her other side and pulled the covers up higher so that just her eyes and nose peeked over the top. Forcing her eyes shut, she made her mind move away from Dan. She wondered what Andrew was hearing about the war, about other lighthouse keepers in Maine and whether they were abandoning their posts.

Somehow, sleep came. And once it did, the night vanished in mere minutes. The morning sun burst in through the cottage windows and forced Elin awake. She was aware as soon as her eyes opened that Dan was downstairs. Her brief flirt with sleep had not erased this knowledge.

She began to pull on the clothes that she had left in a pile the night before. Then she changed her mind and went to her bureau to look for the sweater her Aunt Eleanor had knit for her, and her good slacks. She thought about this, then reason overtook vanity. Guest or no, she had chores to do and she could not work in good clothes. She compromised on a clean pair of dungarees and a pink sweater that had been Sarah's. For a reason she wasn't sure she understood, she put on one blue sock and one pink sock.

Feeling silly for spending so much time on her outfit, Elin yanked her hair into a pony tail and trotted down the stairs. She allowed herself to look quickly in the direction of Andrew and Sarah's room. The door was closed.

In the kitchen, she splashed cold water on her face. Her mind knew that it was morning, but her body was begging her to go back to bed.

She hiked up the tower stairs and extinguished the light. From the lantern room, she watched for a minute as Sailor chased imaginary prey through the tall grass in the clearing. He pounced on the unsuspecting nothing, then trotted away, victorious in his imagination.

When she returned to the kitchen, she pondered her next move. As strange as it felt to be alone, it felt even stranger to have Dan in her house—and without Andrew and Sarah.

Dan should leave the island as soon as possible. Now that she knew that Sarah was doing better, he could go back. She would feed him breakfast as she would any guest, thank him for delivering the message, and send him on his way.

Having finalized her plan, she fired up the stove and heated up a heavy iron frying pan. Then she sliced off hunks of bread and coated them with beaten eggs. As the French toast browned, she expertly flipped the pieces, then stacked them on a plate. As she was scooping the last piece out of the pan, Dan entered the kitchen. His hair was mussed, and he was wearing the same clothes that he had come in last night.

She waited for him to speak first. When he didn't, she thrust a plate toward him. "If you hold this, I'll serve you some French toast," she said stiffly.

"'Morning. Thanks." Dan took the plate. "This looks delicious."

Elin clumsily shoveled the slices onto his plate as if she were a child doing it for the first time. "The jam is . . ." She jerked the spatula toward the table.

"On the table here. I see it. Thank you." He moved toward the table and sat down. Elin busied herself with the stove, then took the frying pan to the sink and began to scrub it.

"Aren't you going to have breakfast?" he asked.

"What's that? Yes, yes, I . . . in a minute." Elin finished scraping the bottom of the pan. She returned to the stove, served herself two pieces of toast, and sat down across from him. She placed a bite of French toast in her mouth and tried to chew without making any sound. Dan was working quickly through his food. For a few long minutes, they ate in silence.

"Why did you get here so late last night?" she blurted out finally. That was not what she had meant to say. She had meant to thank him for coming, but that's not what came out.

"Well, it wasn't so very late, just later than I planned," he began weakly. He looked up at her, then quickly wiped his mouth with his napkin. "Your father had spoken to Ted in the afternoon and by the time I found out and talked him into letting me go in his place—*and* letting me use his boat—it was nearly dark." He paused to wipe his mouth again. "But since his boat has a light on the front, I knew I'd make it out all right."

He looked at her sheepishly. "I didn't mean to frighten you. I'm awfully sorry, really, about that. I talked myself into thinking that I could just sleep on the couch there and give you a hand in the morn—"

"I went to bed a lot earlier than I usually do," she said. "Honestly. I nearly fell asleep reading in the afternoon, and then I did my chores quickly and went to bed. Any other night I would have been awake, and it wouldn't have been so startling."

They each took several bites, waiting to see where the conversation would lead.

"I tell you, I stumbled my way up to the house from the beach with that dog of yours after me the whole way," Dan said at last.

"Sailor."

"He's quite a watchdog, you know."

Elin had to smile at the thought of Sailor doing anything but barking a friendly greeting and wagging his tail. "He always lets us know when something's up." Dan didn't respond, so she found herself continuing to talk. "Of course, we don't have much need for watchdogs around here. I guess we're wasting his talent."

"But if you ever move to town, you'll find that it's mighty useful to—"

"Which we never will." It sounded more defiant than she intended it to.

Dan cleared his throat. "Right," he said. He focused on scraping the last bit of jam off his plate with his fork. Collecting his plate and utensils and hers as well, Dan went to the sink and washed and rinsed the dishes. He set them in the rack to dry and turned expectantly.

"What's on your list of things to do today? Can I help with anything before I go?"

Elin opened her mouth to remind him that he should be leaving but then closed it. After two days of lonely conversations in her head, it was nice to talk to someone. Even a relative stranger. She decided that Sarah would probably approve of his staying until after lunch.

"Well," she began. "Wednesday is the day when Sarah and I mend and iron the clothes that we washed on Monday."

Dan looked concerned. "All right," he began. "Though I've never actually mended or ironed."

Elin laughed. "I was going to say that usually we do that, but with you here, we could help Andrew catch up on some of his chores."

"Great! What was he working on?"

"He was painting the back of the house before Sarah got sick, and that's something he'll need to finish before winter sets in. Paint doesn't hold up too long out here, with the wind and the salty spray."

"Now, painting I'm good at!" he said. "Last summer, I painted our barn. I also re-roofed it if that's anything you need done."

"Oh, no," Elin assured him quickly. "The painting is all that needs to be done. I don't think Andrew wants a new roof."

"All right, then!"

"Just the painting," Elin repeated.

"I'll wash up quick and then you can show me where Andrew keeps his supplies, and maybe an extra old sweater. I think it's cooler today than yesterday."

∿ ∿ ∿

They worked side by side behind the cottage. Elin scraped off the paint where it was peeling, and Dan followed her, slapping paint on the clapboards with gusto. The chore was a distraction from the awkwardness and made conversation come more easily. He talked about the school play that the Drama Club hoped to produce at Christmas time. He wanted to play the lead, but thought it would go to an older boy. He told her about his after-school job and the other characters he worked with at the diner. Elin knew them all by sight and had to laugh at his imitations.

Elin told him about the other people she had met after Andrew had rescued them from various boating mishaps and brought them to the island; some still sent Christmas cards each year. She pointed out her seashell garden. She had wanted a real garden, a bright flower garden that outlined the house, but she couldn't because the soil needed to nourish the plants would be stolen by the wind before the next spring. Instead, she had her shells, and they grew vegetables in buckets filled with good soil from the mainland. She listed the animals they'd kept over the years, and he told about the animals on his farm.

Sometimes they didn't talk at all, but the silence was a comfortable one. By the time the sun was overhead, the back of the house was shining with a new coat of white paint.

As she chipped off the last bit of cracked paint, Elin dropped the scraper on the ground and stretched her arms over her head.

"Oh, boy, my arms ache," she complained cheerfully. She wiggled her fingers. "Fingers are stiff, too."

Dan finished painting, then set his brush down. He reached his hand over and touched the back of it to her cheek. She drew back in alarm.

"I'm sorry," he laughed. "I just wanted to show you how cold my hands are!"

"Oh . . . of course!" She tried to recover quickly. "Mine are nearly frozen, too. Let's go inside and make some hot cocoa!"

"I make the best cocoa," Dan said as he pressed the lid on the paint can and stuck the brush in a jar of turpentine. "I'll bring these and your scraper back to the shed and then meet you in the kitchen. Can we leave the ladder out here?"

Elin considered it. "I'll put that under the passageway. Can't leave it out, so says the Inspector . . . you know, the man who checks on all the lighthouse stations."

"It's heavy. Do you want me to—" Dan looked up at Elin. She stood with her hands on her hips and a slight smile. Dan put up his hands in mock surrender. "Sorry, sorry. I know you can carry it."

∿ ∿ ∿

Elin had just finished setting out the cocoa powder, sugar, and canned milk when Dan came in from outside. He didn't seem nearly as out-of-place in the kitchen as he had first thing in the morning.

"I think Andrew will be pleased to see that job done," he said as he stooped down to untie his boots. "I took another look at it after I went to the shed. We did a good job. Especially at the top there where I had to really stretch."

Elin turned to face him with a smile. "He'll be very happy," she agreed. "He's never been away from the island for more than a few hours, and I'm sure that all of the things he's not doing are weighing on him." Elin gestured toward the counter. "Here's everything you'll need for the cocoa, I think. If you don't mind, I'll just mend this pair of dungarees for Andrew."

"Oh please, go right ahead." Dan stepped over to the counter and pried the top off the container of cocoa with a spoon.

"I'm quite sure the rest of the pile can wait until next week, but I know he'll be looking for these."

"If you're mending, I'll know that you won't be watching me put together my secret recipe. I may want to sell it someday and make lots of money." Dan turned toward Elin with a smile but gave a low whistle when he saw what Elin was doing. "Those pants need more than a few patches, don't they?"

"You know what they say," Elin said as she clenched a needle and thread between her teeth, "'Use it up, wear it out, make it do, or do without.'"

"Who says that?"

"Sarah does. I'll bet most lighthouse families have the same philosophy."

"I see." Dan busied himself mixing and whistling and heating his potion on the stove as Elin took a few expert stitches, pulling the fabric together where it was so thin that it had pulled apart.

"I think these are close to the 'wear it out' part of Sarah's little rhyme," she admitted.

Dan laughed—a nice, low chuckle that made her think of Andrew. He turned from the stove with a cup in each hand. Stepping carefully so as not to spill, he approached the table and set the cups down. "My grandmother taught me how to make hot cocoa," he said. "She tried to teach me how to make her rhubarb pie, too, but I failed miserably."

Elin finished stitching the final tear, tied a quick knot, and bit off the thread with her teeth. She poked the needle into the pin cushion and folded the pants on top of the mending pile. Then she turned her full attention to her cup.

"Mmmmm! This smells wonderful!" She leaned over, drinking in the smell that rose with the wisps of steam. She took a dainty sip, then a bigger gulp. "You're right! This is the best cocoa I've ever had!"

Dan beamed. "I knew you'd like it! Well, I mean I hoped you would."

"Should we have some biscuits as well? And maybe some . . ." she thought for a moment ". . . some soup? I suppose now that we're inside we may as well have lunch."

"That sounds fine."

Elin unwrapped the biscuits she made the day before and heated up a jar of Sarah's famous "Garden Delight" soup. The fall air had provoked their hunger and they ate with gusto. When Elin saw Dan soaking his biscuit in the soup bowl, she decided it would be all right if she did it, too. She had seconds on cocoa, which she could see pleased him.

It took just a few minutes for them to empty their soup bowls. Elin remembered quite suddenly that she had intended to send him off after lunch. She wondered what he planned to do, and what she should say if he left it up to her.

As Elin poked the last chunk of her biscuit into her mouth, Dan leaned across the table and tucked a stray hair into her pony tail. Elin felt her face redden.

"How come you didn't wear your braids?"

Elin tried to read into his question. Was he teasing her about her braids? "My braids . . . ?"

"I liked your braids . . . the last time I was here. Of course, you look fine like this, too." He blushed and then quickly pushed back his chair and stood up. Elin looked at him and wondered who would be the one to say that it was time to go.

"Well," he said.

"Yes?" Elin didn't want him to leave. But she stood up, too.

"It's time—"

"I know." Elin stared at the tablecloth.

"You do?"

"Yes."

"OK, then show me," Dan said, taking a few steps toward the passageway.

"Show you?"

"Yes! The view from the lighthouse. Is that what you were thinking, too?"

Elin laughed with relief and pushed her own chair back so quickly that it nearly tipped over. "Let's go!" she said.

Chapter 9

ELIN PUSHED OPEN the hinged window in the tower and stepped back, indicating to Dan that he should step out.

"Do you think I'll fit?" He looked skeptical.

"Oh, sure," Elin said. "Andrew fits."

"If I get stuck, you're going to have to push me through." He winked at her, and Elin looked away as she felt her face flush.

Dan rubbed his hands together as he assessed the opening. He put one leg outside, then ducked his head and squeezed through, finally standing up on the deck. Elin followed easily, and they stood side by side, holding the delicate railing that encircled the tower. Several comfortable minutes passed as they gazed across the far-stretching water.

"I've never seen the ocean like this, from up high," Dan said at last. "It's certainly impressive, isn't it?"

"You'd love to come up here at night. You can see the stars so brightly: the Big Dipper, the Hunter, the North Star. Andrew's taught me how to find them all. When I was little, I used to make up my own constellations. I think I came up with the Lobster with One Claw and the Dog Scratching His Ear."

"Really!"

"Andrew always tells me how different our night sky is from the one most other people see. He said that in the cities, there are so many lights from cars and houses and street lamps that the sky is faded. Our stars glitter like jewels displayed on black velvet."

"That sounds like something from a poem."

"Oh, Andrew probably made it up. He talks like that sometimes. Like something you'd read in a book. But he is right."

"Mmmm . . ." Dan looked at her. "I can see why you like it out here—on the island, I mean."

"Can you? Really?" Elin wasn't sure he truly understood.

He hesitated as if choosing his words carefully. "I know that most of the time, your days are quiet, and very much the same, which must be comforting. But there's always that element of danger and excitement when you are surrounded by something as unpredictable and powerful as the ocean."

Elin nodded. That was true.

"You know," he continued, "I only live a few miles from the ocean, but it might as well be a hundred. I rarely ever sit near the water and just watch the waves roll in. It's a very soothing sound. Just the rhythm of it, I mean. It's as if the sea is breathing."

"I come up here a lot, even more lately, just to feel the breeze and listen to the water spilling onto the rocks and then going out and repeating it over and over. There's something so satisfying in knowing that nothing can change that. It's always been like that and it always will be." She paused. "Every wave sounds different when it hits, you know, if you really start listening."

Dan waited while several waves came and went far below them. He shook his head and laughed. "I guess you have to come up here a lot to be able to tell one from another."

"I do." Elin lifted her face toward the breeze. "Feel that? Wind's picking up out of the northeast. I don't see any storm clouds, but I wouldn't be surprised if something blew in tomorrow."

"Now, see? If I knew as much as you do about such things, I never would have gotten into trouble on that sailboat!"

"I just listen to Andrew talk about weather all the time."

"I guess it's the most important thing when you live at a lighthouse."

"Pretty much."

Dan shielded his eyes from the sun and surveyed the island. "You can see everything on the island from up here, can't you?"

Elin nodded. "It's not really that big."

"Do you ever . . ." Dan paused, "do you ever feel like it's too small? I mean, I know that you love living out here. But do you feel that you can't get away? What I mean is, sometimes I get on our horse and go riding way into the woods, so far that I think that there's maybe the slightest chance I might have trouble finding my way back. But I like the feeling that the world is so big, and I can go in a lot of directions. Do you know what I mean?"

Elin listened carefully. "I understand," she said simply.

"I'm not saying that the island isn't charming and all."

"I've had dreams. Dreams where I fly away and go to strange places I've read about but never seen. I understand what you mean."

They stood side by side, each thinking private thoughts. The gulls called out from above and waited for answers from the gulls below. The sea air danced around them and the sunlight cut through the chilly air and tried to warm their faces.

Elin pointed to a rock shaped like a ship's hull that jutted into the water on the island's northernmost point. "See that rock over there?"

Dan stood behind her and bent down so that he could follow her finger. "I see the one you mean."

"There's a great story about that rock."

"Tell me."

Elin chuckled as she thought about it and took a moment to redo her windblown ponytail. "Well," she began, "when I was seven, I wrote to the Flying Santa to ask for a doll—"

"The Flying Santa?"

"He's a wonderful old man who drops gifts to lighthouse families from his airplane at Christmas time."

"No kidding!"

"He never forgot me, even when Andrew and Sarah warned me that the weather looked ominous and he might not make it. He always came exactly one week before Christmas Day."

"Now that I think of it, I may have heard of this fellow."

"I wouldn't be surprised. I think he's something of a legend along the New England coast. Anyway, I wrote to him this one year asking for a doll that looked like me, with black hair *in braids*—" She pointed to him as she said that and he grinned. "And eyes that opened and closed and a fancy dress. I remember writing that I had been a very good girl all year, except for when I threw one of the chickens in the water to see if it could swim."

Dan laughed. "And—"

Elin held up one finger. "And in case you're wondering, chickens *can* swim, but they don't like to."

"I guess that's why we have ducks."

"I guess so. So I drew a picture of me holding this doll I wanted, and Andrew took the letter and picture and mailed it to the Flying Santa the next time he was in town. We didn't know his address, but I knew it would get to him.

"Well, the morning he was to fly overhead, I fought with these difficult pieces of driftwood to spell out a giant message in the clearing: HELLO SANTA. It took me nearly all morning because I had refused help from Andrew and Sarah. When I was done, I ran up here to see what it looked like, even though I knew that Andrew wouldn't have wanted me up here. The 'Hello' part was good, but my arms had gotten tired by the time I started on 'Santa.' The letters got smaller and smaller, and the final 'a' looked pretty sad. But I knew the Flying Santa would understand.

"It wasn't long before I saw the speck of plane in the sky, heading for the island. The Flying Santa buzzed the tower first, to let us know the package was coming, and then he returned to drop it. I strained to watch for the box as it fell from the sky. And suddenly there it was—falling, falling, falling and finally bouncing off that very rock and rolling toward the water's edge. I ran down the lighthouse stairs and dashed toward it, shouting, forgetting to wave my thank you. But as I got closer, I saw that the brown wrapping paper was torn, and some of the contents had spilled out.

"I picked up a ball that had rolled under a rock. A package of gum and a box of candy were wedged in a crevice too deep to retrieve. Then I saw my doll. My lovely doll lay crumpled, her eyes closed, the sea washing over her real patent leather shoes. The back of her beautiful braided head was smashed in a hundred pieces. I left her lying there and ran back to the house, crying for my mother and father. Sarah helped me write a note telling the Flying Santa what had happened, and Andrew made a risky trip in a snow squall early the next day to mail it. He knew the doll had to come from Santa.

"On Christmas Eve, as I was helping Sarah arrange Christmas cookies on a plate, we heard a roar and looked out to see a helicopter hovering near the cottage. We ran outside just as it landed in the clearing. It was Santa! He hopped out and handed me a doll wearing a red velvet dress who was holding her own tiny doll dressed just the same. And I was so excited I couldn't even speak. Andrew and Sarah had to thank him for me. I remember they invited him to stay for cookies and tea, but he needed to go because a storm was coming through. I watched that magic machine lift into the sky, and I waved until he was probably landing on the mainland. That was my best Christmas.

Elin stood, lost in the memory. Dan said, "The Flying Santa. Won't that be something to tell your grandkids about when you're all gathered in front of the fireplace in some fancy city skyscraper. They'll never believe it."

Elin thought for a long time before she spoke. "It will be a great story to tell my grandchildren," she said at last.

Dan took a few more steps around the gallery and stopped, looking to the south. "There," he said, pointing. "What's that dark area?"

Elin followed him along the railing to see what he was talking about. "That? Oh, that's where Andrew is digging a big hole so he can bury some broken tools and old pipes. That stuff's too heavy to lug to the mainland to throw away."

"How far has he gotten? Is there much left to be done?"

"Oh, he's about halfway there. He turns everything

into a game, so it takes a little longer, but it's more fun. He was pretending to dig for pirate treasure."

"That sure makes it more interesting."

"It distracts you from your blisters, to be sure."

"Any chance you might really find anything?"

Elin laughed. "Oh, Andrew has a hundred pirate stories, and most of them end with something being buried on this island. He's only told me one or two that I think might have some truth to them."

"How about if I worked on that hole, just to make up for the fact that I'm visiting out here without permission? Maybe Andrew won't be quite so sore at me if he sees how hard I've been trying to help."

For the first time, it occurred to Elin that Dan had taken a risk to come, and then to stay with her. He was going to have to explain to Andrew about bribing Ted, coming out here unannounced, and staying unsupervised.

"I think he would really appreciate it," she said.

"All right, then."

They stepped to the narrow opening and squeezed back into the lantern room. With ease, Elin dropped through the two trapdoors and descended the winding stairs. Dan followed more awkwardly, and tried to catch up with her.

"I'll never get the hang of these steps," he called out cheerfully as he misstepped and pushed against the rounded wall to steady himself.

"Oh, sure you will. You'll get used to it when you've visited the island a few times." Elin heard herself invite him and didn't try to take it back.

She led the way to the shed and found two shovels and two pairs of work gloves. Then they walked through the wind-beaten forest to the pit Andrew had started to dig.

"Boy, it sure looks a lot bigger from down here," Dan said as he stood on the edge looking down. He poked at the unrelenting soil at the ragged rim of the pit. "Tough digging."

"Definitely is," Elin agreed as she jumped down into it. "As it gets deeper, it's even harder because then you have to really struggle to get the dirt out of the hole!" She pointed with the shovel. "See? We've been throwing it out in that direction."

"Okay." Dan joined her in the pit and the two struggled with the rocky soil. After several minutes of steady shoveling, Dan said, "I can see why Andrew comes up with stories to distract the two of you. This is not easy." He grunted under another shovelful. "It's quite a gift, you know, being able to tell a good story. Most people can't do it."

Elin strained to lift another heap of dirt out of the hole. "It comes, I suppose, from not having too many other ways to amuse ourselves out here."

"My family listens to the radio in the evening. I'm not sure any of us would be much good at storytelling. Hey, how about telling me a good pirate story so that I won't dwell on my blisters—and my back."

"All right," Elin thrust the shovel into the dirt and jumped on it to force it down. She scooped up a few rocks and lumps of dirt and managed to get them out of the hole. She jabbed the shovel into the ground again and leaned on the handle.

Thinking back on years of taking in Andrew's tales and embellishing them in her own head, she began to tell the story of Samuel Greene, a New England pirate, one of the fiercest and meanest pirates ever, who, it was said, buried nearly all of his treasure on the barren islands of Maine. She remembered to describe Samuel's girlfriend Elspeth just as Andrew did, with long red hair that she wore in a braid wrapped around her head like a crown.

Dan seemed to take it all in as he continued to work, stopping only to pull Andrew's sweater over his head and toss it away from the hole. He rolled up both sleeves then, and Elin saw the solid forearms of a farm boy. She watched him as he dug firmly into the soil again, then she forced herself back to the story.

As Dan dug and dumped, Elin described the day that Samuel anchored his ship off this very island and came ashore with Elspeth to bury some of his treasure. When he saw another pirate ship approaching, however, he left Elspeth to guard the treasure, and he quickly rowed back to his ship. Elin repeated the warning Samuel shouted to Elspeth as he forcefully rowed the dingy toward the ship: "Stand guard over the treasure until I return."

Dan looked over his shoulder at her. "You sound just like a pirate," he said. "Why, if we get you an eye patch and a peg leg—"

Elin tossed a handful of pebbles at his back. He cried out in good-natured protest, and she scooped up another handful.

"Hey! Sorry!" he laughed. "I love the pirate voice. Keep going!"

Elin told of the battle that broke out between the two pirate ships, and of the way Samuel's ship erupted into flames that lit up the darkening sky. Before long, the fire had consumed the ship, and the charred remains crumbled and sank beneath the waves, taking all those aboard with it.

"And now—" Elin lowered her voice just as Andrew did when he told it. "Her ghost keeps the treasure safe. On nights when lightning makes the sky as bright as the flames did long ago, you can see her, dressed in a long black cloak, her red hair whipping about in the wind, standing here and looking out at the sea, as if she is waiting for her captain to return for her and for his treasure."

Dan had paused for a few minutes to hear the end of the story. When she finished, he shook his head and grinned. "That's a real good story," he said. "Actually gave me shivers."

"Spooky, isn't it?"

"Spooky's the word. You sure you don't want me to stay out here with you for another night?"

Elin scooped up another handful of dirt and threw it hard in his direction. Then, without answering, she tossed her shovel out of the hole and scurried after it.

Chapter 10

"DID YOU GET my letter?"

They were sitting on the back step, watching the chickens hopping about the patch of hardy grass by the clothesline. Elin tossed a few pieces of bread crust toward them, and they all ran forward at once, their plump bodies propelled forward on pairs of skinny legs. She threw another crust out.

"Thanks for helping dig that hole. I do think it's twice as big as it was before. Andrew will be pleased."

"And the letter?"

"I just got it the other day."

Dan looked at her. "And—"

Elin watched the chickens bicker over the bread.

"It was very nice of you to invite me, but . . ."

"But. You're not interested."

"Actually . . ." Elin searched for the right words. "It's not that I wouldn't like to . . . well, with Sarah sick and all, it isn't—"

"I understand."

"It isn't a good time."

Dan looked toward the wharf. Elin waited to hear what he would say next. He stood up and brushed off his pants. It was hopeless; they were caked with dirt and decorated with flecks of white paint.

"Maybe when Sarah is well."

Elin let her silence answer for her.

"I should get going," he said. "I've got to get Ted's boat back to him before it gets dark. I don't have a very good track record with other people's boats, remember?" He smiled, but Elin could see the disappointment in his face.

Elin searched for the words to make him understand. It wasn't that she didn't want to be with him, go with him to a movie, or to ice cream. It was that she, at thirteen almost fourteen, had never gone to school or walked arm-in-arm with a best girlfriend or even *had* a best friend. How could he ever understand that she was more frightened of going to the movies with a group of teenagers than she was of being all alone on the island, with all the responsibilities of a lighthouse keeper?

"I want you to know that it's not that I don't want to spend time with you."

"Oh, sure, I understand."

"No, you don't." Elin flung the rest of the bread crusts so hard that the chickens clucked in annoyance and wobbled down the hill after them. "I have never spent any time with people my own age. I wouldn't know what to—"

"But you did fine today," he protested.

"This, all this, is my . . ." she let her arm sweep across the view and finish her sentence. "As soon as I leave here, everything feels so foreign. I feel so out of place. I've only ever been to town with Andrew."

"It's hard to leave a place that feels safe."

"Yes, it is hard. Even for a short time."

"But it's hard for everybody. Everything worthwhile has some risk to it, don't you think? Why, look at what you and your parents do! Aren't you always taking risks? I mean, it will only get harder to try new things as you get older. Maybe you will live out here forever. But how will you ever be sure that's what you want unless you've known something else? You'll always wonder what else there could have been."

Elin stood up and opened the back screen door. "I don't want to think about it," she said flatly.

"It's not going to be any easier two months from now, or next year."

"Maybe it will." But even as she said it, she knew she wasn't making sense.

"Nope." Dan followed her inside.

"Dan . . ."

"You're afraid."

"I'm not going, is what I was about to say." She stood facing him, arms crossed.

He looked at her, then slowly shook his head. Elin waited to hear what he would say, to see whether he would try to talk her into it. Maybe she didn't feel as certain as she had sounded.

"When my grandmother was thirteen," he began, "she left her family in Poland and came to this country all alone. She put her few things into a trunk, boarded a ship, and headed for America. She spoke no English and had no one waiting for her here. All she had was the name of a second cousin that her mother had scribbled for her on a piece of paper and instructions to try to find her somewhere in New York. Imagine that—leaving parents and sisters and brothers and a home behind because she knew that there would be so many more opportunities for her in this country."

"What happened to her?" Elin asked.

"She got a job working in a hotel from what I understand," he said. "I don't know that she was able to find her relatives in New York. But she worked hard and saved her money and eventually moved to the outskirts of Boston. She bought her own house, married, and had a family. Her husband, my grandfather, had come from Poland, too. He started a window-washing business and did very well. All of her five children went to college, which was quite something in those days. Her oldest daughter, my mother, graduated from Mt. Holyoke and taught school until she married my father. And now I have all sorts of opportunities because of what my grandmother did sixty years ago."

Elin considered his story as she watched him remove his boots, cross the kitchen, and disappear into the living room. She waited, unsure how to respond. She knew that what he said made sense. She also knew that she didn't want to hear it. Not now.

He reappeared. "I left Andrew's sweater on the bed," he said. "I should probably get going now."

Elin nodded slowly. She wished that he wasn't leaving right now, when things were strained between them. But instead of saying that, she said, "You probably should."

In silence, they walked across the island to the wharf. Elin watched as he struggled to untie the knots he had made the night before. It seemed like he had been there so much longer than just a day. Elin tried to put a good sentence together in her head, one that would describe how much she enjoyed his company, how much she hoped he would come back for a visit. But nothing sounded right in her mind, so she didn't try to say it aloud.

As he finally flipped the ropes into the boat, she said, "Andrew will be grateful for everything you did."

"That's good. I'm glad I could help." He shifted to the back of the boat and yanked the cord to start the small motor. The engine sputtered and died. Elin tried to will it broken so that he could stay longer and they could make things right between them, but with another tug the motor buzzed into life.

Dan raised one hand in a quick wave and guided the boat away from the dock. Elin stood without moving as the boat moved farther and farther away. Finally the sound of the splashing waves overtook the whine of the motor, and the boat dissolved into a black dot.

Elin turned and walked slowly back toward the house. If only she could have made Dan understand that her life had always been so calm until now. Ever since he came into her life and they made the trip to Rock Point to bring him back, everything had become chaotic and uncertain.

She walked through the kitchen and into her parents' bedroom for a reason she didn't really understand. Dan had made the bed neatly and left Andrew's sweater folded up at the foot of it. She sat down on the edge and sighed. Why did life have to be so complicated?

～ ～ ～

Elin's stomach didn't want dinner, but her head wasn't ready to sleep. She stoked the fire in the cookstove and dumped in the last of the coal. She lit the lamp on the kitchen table and took it into the living room.

She had taken care of the light without really thinking about it, one-half hour before dusk, as always. She had climbed the stairs without counting them and left the lantern room without dreaming.

On the coffee table was *Grimm's Fairy Tales*. She carried it up to her room. When she set the lamp on her nightstand, it made a cozy circle of light on her pillow and the top of her bedcovers. She didn't feel like changing into her pajamas and so she didn't, but she pulled the covers over her clothes and stuffed both pillows behind her. She turned to the story of Snow White and Rose Red, her favorite, and counted on it to take her back—back to the years when everything was simple and the same.

Soon the familiar words soothed her, chasing away thoughts of Dan, of being without her parents, of the war everyone was talking about. The fable drew her in, and she was Rose Red, at first frightened by the monstrous bear that appeared at her door, then relieved to find out that he was gentle and harmless. Pictures played in her mind as a wicked gnome berated the kind sisters until at last the bear killed him with one blow. As clearly as if it were happening in her own room, Elin saw the bear magically transformed into a handsome prince.

As the sisters rode off to the castle with the prince and his handsome brother, an explosion jolted Elin out of her magical world. From somewhere across the waves came a noise like thunder but deeper. It came up through Elin's entire body and made her shudder. A long, low rumble that ended in a muffled bang echoed over and over across the water.

Her heart stopped beating for a minute, then resumed at breakneck speed. She knew every island sound by heart: every gull's cry, the variations in every breath of wind. She knew the different drumming noises made by the rain as it hit the tin roof of the chicken coop or the shingles capping the cottage or the tower windows. She knew them all.

And she knew this sound, though she had never heard it, the same way she identified the strange staccato chopping of the helicopter that had brought the Flying Santa so many years before. She knew that this sound had to be an enemy torpedo, just like at Cape Henry.

A submarine was out there somewhere, too close. Someone was shouting orders in foreign words to others who wanted to fight with Americans. Elin's skin turned damp and cold and her breath came in short gasps. She felt like the fish Andrew caught and tossed on the shore, mouths opening and closing without getting a breath, eyes wide and unblinking.

But as the dark echoes faded, she questioned herself. Had she really heard something? Or had she imagined it? Had she dozed off as she—

BOOM!

This time the house shuddered with her. As she sat, frozen, waiting for the echoes to subside, every sound became amplified. Even the ticking of the clock in the hallway ricocheted off the walls like gunfire.

When a few minutes passed with no blast, she crept to the window and peered into the purple light of near-darkness. The silhouette was familiar: the chicken house in front of the tree with a branch bent like a rainbow, the cluster of pines that bordered the shoreline. It looked serene as always. And yet . . .

Elin turned around and slid down the wall until she was as small as she could be. Instead of feeling safe within the island shores, protected as she always had, she suddenly felt very trapped. And so very much alone.

She wanted to get away, to get to town, to find Andrew. She wanted to get off the island. But Andrew had the boat, and Dan was probably already in the harbor or close to it. And even if she dared take the rowboat, it would take every bit of strength she had to row all the way to shore, and in the dark no less. And somewhere out there the submarine was slipping below the water's surface, silent and unseen, like an evil ghost. No, she couldn't leave.

As she stumbled back into bed, her heart was beating so hard that it felt as if it was inside her head. Bang, bang,

bang, bang! Was that her heart or more torpedoes? She couldn't tell.

She pulled the covers up as high as they would go, trying to chase away the chill she felt. Even under her heavy blankets, she shook uncontrollably. After a minute, she reached over and turned out the lantern. She felt safer blending in with the gray hues of twilight. Had people on shore heard it? Did anyone know what was happening? Did Andrew and Sarah know she was in trouble?

She sat in bed, tense, taut, focusing on the sound of the wind and the waves, usually so comforting, but tonight somehow sinister, telling tales of demons and evil spirits. The gusts made the house groan and complain, and every rattle could have been German soldiers pulling on the door or peering in the windows. Could submarines land like motor boats or sailboats? Could a submarine land on the beach, could the top hatch open up and could dozens of soldiers pour out like the bubbly foam from an over-shaken bottle of root beer?

The harder she strained to listen, the more confused she became. What was that creak? And that tapping? Did she hear voices? She fell back on her pillow, her mind whirling, her room spinning around and around as if she was being tossed about the waves during a hurricane.

She wanted to go to sleep so that when she woke up, it would all be over. But she was afraid to sleep. She listened to the clock in the hall. She counted the seconds—fifty-eight, fifty-nine, sixty. Had that just been one minute? The night would never end. It seemed like hours since she had heard the explosions. Or had it been mere minutes?

The more she struggled not to, the more she pictured swarms of soldiers scaling the rocks rimming the island. Her dizzy head spun desperate, crazy tales of escape. She could become tiny and crawl under a tea cup where no one would find her. Or she could sprout wings and fly off into the night like a bird, soaring over the black waves into the hospital room where Andrew and Sarah were. They would pull her to them, wrap their arms around her, and keep her safe. But when she re-emerged from these dreams, the terror returned like a wave crashing into a reef.

Through her window, she saw that the sky had turned black. So time was going by after all, the night wouldn't last forever. As she stared at the night sky, a horrifying thought formed in her mind. The light. Its beam burned bright, beckoning the enemy soldiers to the island! What had the Coast Guard officer said? It silhouetted the ships and made it easier for the submarines to find them!

She slipped out of bed and made her way through the darkness to the passageway, and then to the lighthouse and up the fifty-two steps. She tried to step quietly, but somehow the blackness made every noise so much sharper. She pulled herself into the lantern room and stepped toward the light, ready to extinguish the flame.

But then she hesitated. To turn it off would be to condemn ships to crash into the submerged ledges. And yet to keep it shining would mean that the submarines would have easy targets. Panic overwhelmed her as she tried to think of some way to help the ships to pass by safely.

As she stood there, stiff with indecision, she looked across the clearing and thought she saw something move. She reached for the binoculars and focused on the shape. A figure was stumbling across the lawn! She felt her breath cut off just for an instant, and then she relaxed. This was not the stealthy stalking of someone who was unsure where he was headed. The dark figure was racing clumsily, purposefully, for the house. And something about the way he ran was familiar.

Revived, she left the light on for now and dropped through the set of trapdoors to the stairs. Nimbly descending the stairs, she hurried through the passageway and burst through the kitchen door.

"HEY!" someone hollered out as he fell backward into the living room.

"Dan?" Elin asked, rushing to his side. "It's just me, Elin!"

"Oh, for Pete's sake." Dan rolled onto his side and pushed himself to a sitting position. "You nearly scared me to death."

Elin had to smile despite her concern. "Now we're even," she said. "How did you know to come back?"

"I heard your emergency cannon. I was nearly to shore when I heard it. I wasn't sure whether I should go and get help, or come myself, but I figured it would be a lot quicker if I just came back."

Shaking her head, Elin swallowed hard and gripped his arm. "That wasn't our cannon," she said.

"It wasn't?"

"No. It was a torpedo. From a German sub."

"What?!"

"It had to be."

"How do you know for sure?"

"What else would make a noise like that, way out here? When we were in town a month or so ago to bring you and Jack home, a man from the Coast Guard told us that German subs had been spotted close to the East Coast."

"But that seems so hard to believe. The war's way over in Europe, after all."

"I guess it's not anymore. Someone, I can't remember who, said that the submarines are trying to disrupt our shipping routes."

Dan rubbed his eyes as he tried to take it all in. "It could be, I guess," he admitted. "It's just so hard to believe.

Well, then, that makes the decision easy. Come on, let's go." Dan stood up and brushed himself off, but Elin remained crouching. He put his hand out to her, but she ignored it.

"Where are you going?" Elin asked.

"To Rock Point. What do you mean 'where'?"

"Dan, I can't leave here. There'll be no one to take care of the light."

Dan threw his hands into the air in disbelief. "Are you crazy? If there are German subs shooting torpedoes out here, who cares about the damn light?" He caught his mistake and muttered, "Excuse my language" before he continued.

"Elin, no one—not Andrew, not that Inspector fellow you're always talking about, not Sarah—no one will be upset with you for leaving. In fact, I'm going to guess that they will all be upset if you stay, given the circumstances!"

Elin rose slowly and pushed herself a little taller onto her toes so that she was looking more evenly at Dan. "Dan, the light has never been left unattended. You don't understand—"

"I understand that if what you're saying about torpedoes is true, then you don't have a choice. You have to leave."

Elin folded her arms across her chest in defiance. "I won't."

"You will leave, or else . . ." Dan searched for an appropriate consequence. "You'll really wish you had. Because I am leaving. It is absurd to stay out here when the enemy—the Germans, for crying out loud—are out there!" He walked toward the door, glancing over his shoulder at her. "You're not going to stay here by yourself."

Elin watched him go. "That's up to you," she said. "I'm going to stay. This isn't about staying forever . . ." She paused for emphasis. "It's just about staying tonight."

"So the two of us should stay out here in the middle of . . . of who knows what?"

Elin unfolded her arms and rubbed distractedly at her mouth and chin. Dan stood frozen by the back door, his hand holding the screen door ajar.

"With the two of us . . ." Elin began to pace the kitchen floor, her head bowed, thinking aloud. "The light silhouettes ships . . . and makes them easier for subs to hit . . ."

"What?" Dan nearly shouted. "Elin, are you hearing yourself? Turn out the light, and let's get off this island!"

"Wait!" It was more of an appeal than an order. Elin went to Dan and held onto his arm firmly.

"Just let me think this through," she said. "Hear me out and see what you think."

She released his arm and began to pace again.

"What about shipwrecks? If we turn out the light, who knows how many ships might stray near the ledges? This is the time when all the ships from Nova Scotia are bringing apples to—"

"The moon's out; it's a clear night," Dan interrupted. His hand was still holding the door. "The crew on those ships can see what's ahead."

"The ledges, the reefs, they're underwater. The men on those ships rely on the light. They know where they are when they see it." Elin twirled to face Dan. "What was the first thing you said?"

Dan wrinkled his face in concentration. "I don't know. It's a clear night?"

"That's it!" Elin jabbed her finger toward him. "That's how we'll do it! I'll turn out the light and watch for ships from the tower. When I see one, I'll signal you . . . somehow. We'll have to figure that out . . . and you can blow the foghorn, the siren! That way everyone on the boats will know that they're near the island!"

Dan was shaking his head. "It just doesn't seem smart to stay out—"

"Dan, I can't do this by myself." Elin took a step toward him and held him firmly by both arms so that he had to look at her. "Someone has to be in the tower and someone else has to be by the siren. That's on the other side of the island. You need to help me."

Dan looked into her eyes as she pleaded with him. After a long moment of deliberation, his hand fell from where it was holding open the door and the door snapped shut.

"I know I'm going to wish I had gone back," he sighed, shaking his head. Elin gave him a brief hug and stepped back to outline her plan.

"I'll show you where the foghorn is and how to operate it. I hope I can remember how Andrew does it. I'm nearly certain I remember. Then I'll go into the tower and use the binoculars to scan the water. When I see a ship, I'll let you know by . . ." Her voice trailed off as she glanced quickly around the room. Her gaze fell on the hooks near the back door. She stepped over and grabbed a whistle hanging on a length of twine. "I'll blow this whistle."

Dan studied it doubtfully. "Are you sure I'll be able to hear it?"

"I'm sure. When I was little, Sarah made me wear it all the time. If I ever got into trouble, I was supposed to blow it. Andrew tried it out first, to make sure that Sarah could hear it from anywhere on the island."

Dan fingered it, then looked at Elin with a grin. "Did you ever need to use it?"

Elin grinned back. "Nope. I always got myself out of trouble. I'll blow once when the ship comes close enough to be able to hear the horn, and then I'll give two blasts when it has passed the island and is out of danger."

Dan took in a deep breath and waited a long time before he let it out.

"All right," he said after a pause. "Show me this foghorn."

The lantern lit their way along the path behind the house and shed to the building perched on the edge of the northern bluff that housed the fog siren. Elin led the way inside.

She held up the lantern to reveal the massive coal-fired boiler that fed the horn outside.

Dan whistled as he stepped into the building.

"Are you sure you know how this thing works?" he asked.

"I'm sure." Elin tried to sound more confident than she felt. "This is one of the older signals around. I know that Andrew has talked about getting it replaced with something more modern. It breaks down a lot and the parts are hard to get. I suppose no one will bother replacing it now . . ." Her voice trailed off as she studied the boiler.

"The fire—the coal and matches are stored over there—creates steam that is forced out through those disks and then through that thing that looks like a trumpet aiming toward the water," she explained. "It's just about the worst sounding thing you could ever imagine, but it's much more effective than bells or whistles, especially way out here. But you can't imagine what it's like trying to sleep with this thing going off all night."

Dan nodded as he began to tug and push at the various handles on the boiler.

"You'll have to be mindful of the steam," Elin warned. "You have to regulate the fire and water supply carefully. You can't leave it, even for a minute."

Dan was scrutinizing the mechanisms. "I know how this works," he said finally. "I can get this thing going."

Elin felt a surge of optimism. "When I blow—" she began, but was interrupted by a deep blast that echoed across the ocean over and over. Alarmed, Elin grabbed Dan's arm without thinking about it. As the echoes faded, she noticed and released her grip.

"They're still out there," she said. "It sounds even closer than before."

Dan was still. "I wonder if we'll be drawing attention to ourselves by sounding this siren," he said, almost to himself.

"We can't think about that," Elin said. "We really don't have a choice." She stepped back and eyed the boiler, hoping it was up to the task.

BOOOOM! And again, BOOOOM!

They both jumped, then stared at each other as the thunderous sounds faded away, little by little, finally overtaken by the sound of the waves. Elin shook her head in disbelief and let a smile flicker across her face.

"What in the world are you smiling about?" Dan asked.

"I was just thinking of what Andrew will say. He's lived out here for so many years, never having missed a night, and look what happens when he's on shore. He won't believe it!"

"I can't quite believe it myself. Maybe I'll be able to get extra credit in current events class for this, if I live to tell the story." He put his hand on Elin's shoulder. "You take your position up in the tower, captain, and I'll get this boiler fired up."

Elin nodded. She left him with the lantern and relied on the moonlight to guide her back toward the house. She slipped into the passageway and felt her way up the tower stairs, letting her hands run across the black walls.

The fierce brightness of the lantern room shocked her into a squint. She located the binoculars and put them around her neck. Silently reassuring herself of the sound-ness of her plan, she reached over and extinguished the light.

Immediately, the blackness closed in around her, chok-ing her, wrapping her so tightly she could hardly breathe. She fought to stay calm. She waited, knowing that the darkness would release its grip. Soon her eyes were able to see shapes, light and dark, and then finally make out fuzzy details nearby as the black evaporated into gray.

She began her slow march around the lantern room, watching the white-crested waves shimmering in the moonlight. She wondered what Dan was thinking. Was he wishing that he hadn't listened to her and had gone back? Or was he wishing he hadn't come back at all? She smiled ruefully. He's probably wishing he hadn't bribed Ted in the first place, she thought.

She scanned the horizon with her binoculars. Nothing. She walked first in one direction around the room, then the other. Time moved slowly, and the moon crawled across the sky in its familiar arc. She wished that she had a clock with her. It seemed as if hours had passed, but she knew that they hadn't. Her eyes grew weary with the strain of staring into the binoculars.

She wondered if Dan had the fire going in the boiler. Coal fires were tricky. Should she check and make sure he was ready? As she pondered this, she lifted the binoculars and peered toward the open sea.

A ship! A ship was heading in her direction! She waited for just a minute, to be sure it wouldn't change its course, and then she let the binoculars swing while she pushed at the glass door and slipped outside. She leaned as far over the railing as she dared and blew hard on the whistle.

The shrill blast hung on the air. Elin waited for the siren to respond. Seconds passed, then minutes. She moved around the tower to look once more through the binoculars. The ship was cutting quickly through the water, heading for the island at an alarming pace.

Elin gulped. Why wasn't Dan working the siren? Was it broken? Should she re-light the wick and let the flashing light warn those on the ship? Which was a bigger threat to those on board: the reefs or the submarine . . . or submarines? Andrew would have known what to do. She wasn't sure.

She waited for the siren. Nothing. Seconds stretched by. Still nothing. She lit a match and reached toward the wick, then the fog siren screamed. The piercing noise sliced through the ocean's song like a sharp sword. With relief, she shook out the flame.

Again the siren blared out its warning. Even though Elin was expecting it, she jumped. She squinted through the binoculars. The ship appeared to be turning . . . or was it just that she was seeing what she wanted to see? If her decision to turn out the light was a poor one, and lives were lost as a result of it, she would live the rest of her life revisiting that crucial moment and wishing she had made a different choice.

The siren shrieked again. Repositioning herself, she watched to see where the ship was headed. It took endless minutes before she knew for sure. The ship had turned away from the island and the underwater reefs, and the danger of a shipwreck off her shore.

Relief came to her in waves, each one surer than the one before. She gave two blasts on the whistle to convey the good news to Dan. They had done it! Her plan had worked! But the triumphant lull was short-lived. Another torpedo blast shattered her brief rest, and she leaped to attention once more.

Twice more that night the submarine aimed at some unknown target and fired, and three more times ships approached and then were turned away by the forceful message of the fog siren.

It wasn't until the first pale hint of daylight that Elin gave herself permission to relax. As she did, the exhaustion of the long, tense night pressed on her like a suit of armor. Her eyes began to burn and her legs felt unsteady.

A sliver of sun appeared on the faraway horizon. As it inched upward, it splashed an orange tint on everything in sight. On a normal morning, she would be extinguishing the light right now.

The tide was coming in. Waves greeted the rocky shore and then pulled back for another enthusiastic greeting. Sailor was leaping in abandon after an imaginary creature. The cottage looked as snug as always from high above. At the briefest glance, everything looked the same.

But as Elin stood staring out of the lantern room, she saw it all very differently. Now the chicken coop was a place she might hide if anyone came onto the island. The boathouse would be a place to wait until it was safe to jump into the boat and speed for the mainland. From the cliffs on the western shore she might be able to signal for help. It didn't really look the same at all.

She heard a thud below her and reached down to pull open the trapdoor. Dan lifted himself through with effort and then let the door fall back into place.

"Good job," he said. He patted her back with a hand blackened from coal dust.

"You, too."

They stood together looking out at the sea, thinking of the secrets it was keeping and knowing that from then on, nothing would be the same.

Chapter 11

"It's only a matter of time before it's official." The Coast Guard officer drummed his fingers on the kitchen table and tilted his head as if trying to read Andrew's eyes. But Andrew stared into his coffee cup. Elin watched and listened from the doorway.

"We will be involved in this war sooner or later, Andrew, you know that. And I'm thinking it will be sooner. Your daughter here—" he stopped drumming and gestured toward Elin, "—can likely back me up on that one."

His words hung heavily in the air.

Andrew released a sigh that made his coffee ripple. When it was still again, he looked up. But still he didn't speak. The officer cleared his throat, then folded his hands deliberately in front of him and slowly squeezed them together. He continued.

"They're all being darkened, closed up. Every lighthouse on the East Coast. For the safety of the keepers and their families, and for national security. Orders are coming out of Washington. I am truly sorry, folks. I know this is difficult to hear."

Andrew nodded as if his head suddenly weighed too much.

how about some of this coffee cake? I made it earlier and it's still warm."

"Sit, Sarah. Sit down. Don't be rushing around so." Andrew pushed at the chair next to his so that the seat welcomed her. She ignored it and remained standing.

"So that's one option you have," Jim continued. "Now there's always factory work, too. The war may mean quite a few more factory jobs opening up in Northfield and Medville."

Andrew looked glum at Jim's mention of factory work. Seeming to sense Andrew's mounting unhappiness, Jim turned to Sarah.

"Sarah, I believe you'll enjoy the company of the ladies in town," he went on brightly. "My wife Joan organizes teas and card games and all sorts of social things for her group of lady friends. I'm sure you'll hook right up with some ladies in your new neighborhood."

"What a useful way to pass the time." Sarah looked at Jim with a weak smile. "I . . . I apologize for my sarcasm. I don't mean to sound rude. But my work here is so worthwhile. I'm not sure I want to spend my days gossiping and playing cards."

"Yes, I do understand what a change it will be, how difficult it will be for you all," Jim said. He seemed to have run out of things to say.

Elin suddenly felt sorry for him. She could tell that he was trying to paint dismal news in as positive a light as he could. It wasn't his fault, after all, that they had to move, and he really wasn't obligated to do anything more than deliver the orders and leave. He was doing his best to cheer them up.

Elin stepped into the room and moved close to the table. "It wouldn't be my choice to move to town under other circumstances," she said slowly. "But these are not ordinary times. And the decision has been made for us, so we'll have to make the best of it.

"But there's one thing I know, and that is that Andrew does not belong on a fishing boat. He would hate that, and we'd hate being apart from him for weeks at a time. And a factory job would be unbearable for someone like him." She reached out and put her hands on Andrew's shoulders. "You know what you should do, Andrew? You should be a teacher. You really should! You made every subject exciting for me, even history. You'd enjoy it, too."

Andrew waved away the idea. "I'm not qualified to teach in a real school, Ellie. Teaching my own daughter is one thing. But no bonafide school is going to want—"

"Now, don't be so sure." Jim seemed eager to grab onto Elin's suggestion. "I know the headmaster at a small day school in Hamden, just ten miles or so south of Rock Point. He grew up next door to me. We were buddies all through grade school. I will speak to him if you'd like."

"Andrew would be wonderful with children." Sarah still hadn't put down the coffee cake. "Why, Elin always tests far ahead of others her age, just because of what Andrew does with her."

"So I don't get any of the credit?" Elin gave Sarah a playful poke. Sarah uncharacteristically returned it with her free hand.

"I suppose it's worth looking into." Andrew leaned back in his chair and a slight smile crossed his lips. "I'd enjoy being with young people. Did well in school myself."

"You graduated first in your class," Sarah said.

"Class was only fourteen kids, Sarah." Andrew sent her a grin. "But I did like school, loved learning new things—

especially love history. Well, yes then, if you would look into that possibility for me, Jim, I'd appreciate it." He leaned forward and drank the rest of his coffee in a single gulp. "All right, Sarah," he said. "I'll have a piece of that coffee cake now."

~ ~ ~

Even though Elin tried to hold back the time by paying attention to every minute of every day, three weeks swiftly passed. Andrew was especially quiet during those days, spending most of his time in the lantern room. He did seem briefly invigorated by a letter from Jim with information about a meeting with the headmaster at the Groton Point Day School. But his enthusiasm quieted after a day or two, and his general melancholy was hard for him to disguise.

He'd found a house for them to rent on the outskirts of Rock Point, a caretaker's cottage that was part of a dairy farm. When he knew where he would be working, then they could buy their own house with the extra money the government had given them and really settle down.

Sarah, meanwhile, focused on the most minute details of cleaning the house and packing. Every piece of Andrew's family china was washed and dried and painstakingly wrapped in newspapers before being tucked into a wooden crate. Elin thought the attention to every cup and saucer was unnecessary for the china, but probably necessary for Sarah, who, when she wasn't trying to distract the others with food, was trying to distract herself with busyness.

The boat arrived early on an October morning, the coldest morning they'd had since the previous spring. The Coast Guard sent two young men to help Andrew move the furniture. Because Andrew had been bringing boxes of clothes and dishes and books to the mainland nearly every day for two weeks, only the largest items and a few personal things were left.

Andrew's gloom retreated behind a colonel's facade as he directed the moving of the living room sofa and chair, the kitchen table and chairs, the beds and bureaus and rugs, and the steamer trunks. The men soberly followed his orders. It seemed to Elin that they sensed how painful the move was for Andrew and tried especially hard to please him. With the utmost care, they moved each piece of furniture out through the front door and across the yard, responding quickly to Andrew's commands to "watch that corner of the table" or "mind the step there."

Elin tried to stay out of the way. She had helped Sarah pack up the last trunk hours earlier, and there was nothing she could do to help with the furniture. Or nothing the men would let her do, anyway.

When the men finally headed up the stairs to Elin's room to move the last pieces, she wandered through the empty rooms downstairs. She clattered across the bare floor in the hallway, her footsteps echoing strangely. In the living room, dents marked where the legs of the sofa had pushed into the soft pine floor for so many years. She could see the faintest outline where the rug had been. Sunlight filtering through the curtains had lightened the floor around it and left behind what looked like the ghost of a rug.

The kitchen didn't feel like theirs anymore. Without Sarah setting a pie on the windowsill to cool and Andrew leaning against the counter with his cup of coffee, without Franklin the seagull twirling over the sink, it could have been anyone's kitchen with honey-colored pine floors and white-washed cabinets.

When she heard Andrew tell the men, "This is it, boys, the last item," she waited until they went outside, then she walked back through the living room and climbed the stairs. As she did, she ran her fingers along the wall where the photographs of Sarah's father and mother had hung. Andrew had neatly patched the nail holes, though for what reason Elin did not know.

At the top of the stairs, she peeked into her room. It looked so much smaller with no furniture. She wondered how that could be. As she ran her fingers lightly across the painted walls, she stopped when she got to a pencil mark near the door that she had made when she was barely five years old. Tracing around the wobbly letter "E," she remembered how Sarah had scolded her when she had discovered it. She'd called Andrew upstairs in the hopes that he would mete out an appropriate punishment, but, much to Sarah's dismay, Andrew couldn't contain his delight. He had been trying to teach Elin how to write her name for a week, and he was exceedingly pleased that she had mastered the first letter. Sarah must've noticed it when she was cleaning and left it there on purpose, perhaps as a simple reminder of the girl who had grown up here.

Elin went back down the stairs and out through the front door, which had been propped open. She paused by her seashell garden, then stooped down and dug out her favorite, the barely pink corkscrew shell with the ruffled edges. After brushing away the dirt, she tucked it into the pocket of her jacket.

As she walked across the front yard, she looked up at the house. She had thought that she would feel sorry for it, that she would almost be able to hear it pleading with her to stay. But the curtainless windows stared vacantly at her. The house didn't speak to her at all.

Elin ducked into the passageway and headed up to the lantern room, paying deliberate attention to each step. *Dix-*

huit had a small wedge-shaped piece missing from the corner. She didn't want to forget that.

Once there, she immediately slipped through the hinged window that opened onto the gallery. Gripping the narrow railing, she made several careful steps to the right so that she faced the open sea. She barely noticed the biting autumn wind whipping her hair and yanking at her clothes.

She stared out at the view that made the world feel so vast, so infinite and unbounded. She shut her eyes and tried to keep the vision from escaping. She had to take this picture with her and be able to recall it when she needed to revisit the island in her thoughts.

And the sounds. She wanted to remember the way the waves rumbled as they rolled toward the island and finally exploded on the rocks. The high-pitched scolding of the gulls when Sarah was not tossing the fish heads to them fast enough. The never-ending rush of the wind. She wanted to remember the way the wind kept everything in constant motion as it danced through the tall, stiff grass and made the stubby pine trees shudder. She soaked it all in, every sensation, every sound, every sight.

In the periodic lull between the waves, Elin could hear the men calling to each other near the dock. She stepped carefully around the gallery so that she could watch what they were doing. The taller of the two men was strapping down the last piece of furniture—Elin's bureau—while the other man stood on the dock, unwinding the ropes from the pier and tossing them onto the deck of the boat.

Andrew watched them, his hands on his hips. As soon as the second man had jumped onto the boat, Andrew leaned over and gave the boat a hard shove. It drifted for a minute, then Elin heard the engine kick in, and the boat surged forward. Andrew lifted his hand in a brief wave but didn't move from the end of the dock. He stayed and watched the boat as it shrank toward the far-off coast. At last he turned and slowly made his way along the rugged strip of land that edged the island. Elin lost sight of him when he reached the pine forest. She tried peering through the trees to catch a glimpse of him, but it was no use.

Elin suddenly wondered where Sarah had gone. She hadn't seen her for at least an hour. She stepped around the gallery, scanning the island for the unmistakable blue of Sarah's coat. She felt worry begin to overtake her, and then there she was. There was Sarah, standing on the island's eastern ridge, near the spot where Andrew had pulled Elin ashore as an infant. She was standing absolutely still, looking out to sea. Elin wondered what she was thinking, what memories she was trying to take away with her.

Elin turned to see Andrew making his way through the tall grass and then across the front of the house. She watched as he disappeared through the kitchen door.

The rush of the wind and waves overwhelmed the sound of him climbing the tower stairs and opening and closing the trapdoor to the lantern room. But even without turning to look, Elin knew he was there.

Andrew worked his large frame through the hinged window. Moving close to Elin, he reached over and took her hand. They stood together, looking beyond Sarah to the open sea, toward far distant shores where a battle raged that was spreading across the world.

Finally Andrew said, "Time to go, Ellie."

～ ～ ～

Andrew handed Elin a large, thin package wrapped in brown paper after she'd stepped into the boat. Sarah was already settled in the middle seat.

"Keep this from getting wet," he said. "It's precious."

"What is it?" Elin squeezed the paper for a clue.

"You can tear a tiny piece off the corner and take a look if you'd like," Andrew said. Elin saw a twinkle in his eye, something she hadn't seen in many weeks.

"Andrew, what . . . ?"

"Go ahead, you can peek."

Elin tugged at the tape on the corner and tore off a strip of the brown paper. She turned to Andrew with a wide grin. "Andrew! The painting of me! How did you get it back?"

"No one bought it, Ellie. I couldn't bear to leave it with Stan, so I brought it back here the same day. I was going to save it for your birthday, but I figured that maybe today . . ." He looked at her and she saw tears shining in his eyes.

She leaned over and hugged him tightly.

"Hey, no rocking the boat, now," he said as he returned her squeeze.

"Thank you so much, Andrew. You know how much I love it."

She sat down in the bow of the boat and balanced the package on her knees. "Now when I tell my grandchildren about growing up on this island, I'll be able to show them something to go along with my stories."

"Well, I'm just glad you inspired me to paint it, Rapunzel."

"Oh, Andrew!"

"Did you remember to contact the Wilsons about leaving us the key?" Sarah asked.

Andrew reached into his pocket, then held up a key for her to see. "We're all set," he said. "I stopped by his office the last time I was in town. Made sure Elin's room was going to get a fresh coat of paint before we moved in and paid the first three months rent, too."

Andrew untied the boat and hopped into the back. With an oar, he pushed away from the dock. As they drifted for a second or two, he turned and looked at the island.

"Ready?" He looked at Sarah, then Elin.

Sarah lifted her head up high and nodded.

"Ready," Elin said.

He yanked on the cord and the boat roared to life. He steered away from the island.

Elin twisted around so that she faced forward. She resisted the urge to look back.

She stared ahead at the familiar bumpy line that was the coast of Maine. This was the way she had seen the mainland every day for thirteen, almost fourteen years. What would it be like, she wondered, a year from now, or ten years from now, to have become used to seeing the island from far away—as a swollen line on the horizon?

She let her mind imagine what it must have been like for Dan's grandmother on her journey across the ocean alone, with just one trunk holding all of her belongings and no mother or father to take care of her. How must she have felt as she watched the shores of her homeland fall farther and farther away? And when, after weeks of riding ocean swells within the cramped belly of the ship, she reached America and disembarked and greeted her new country all by herself, how brave she must have been.

The trip to Rock Point seemed so much shorter than usual. As they slipped into the harbor, Elin imagined the familiar embrace as the points of land reached out to hug them. She looked for the boat that held their furniture but didn't see it. Andrew chugged toward the docks and Elin watched for an open slip. When she saw one, she turned to him and pointed. He nodded and steered the boat toward it.

As they got closer, Elin set the painting aside and stood up, gathering the rope that lay at her feet. She tossed the looped end and ringed one of the piles that propped up the pier, then she pulled the boat in and secured the knot. From the corner of her eye, she saw someone coming toward them.

"You timed your arrival perfectly. We just got here. Boat with your things is way across the harbor." Dan was bounding down the wharf. It shook under his heavy steps.

Elin turned to Andrew. "How did—?"

"Dan and Ted will help us unload the furniture and bring it to the house. Ted offered to let us use his truck the last time I was in town. And they'll help with any cleaning we need to do before we can move the furniture in."

Elin nodded. "I see."

She poised herself to step out of the boat and glanced up to see Dan offering her his hand. She hesitated, then grabbed it, and let him pull her onto the wharf.

"You're pretty strong, for a guy." She smiled at him. He returned the smile.

"Pass me my painting, Andrew," she said.

He did. She tucked it under her arm and walked along the dock, away from the boat and toward a new life.

Elin's Island
Historical Note

Though Elin and her family and friends are fictitious characters, her story is based on the lives and experiences of real lighthouse families and events that actually took place.

Most lighthouse families from Elin's time enjoyed a comfortable (if monotonous) existence. Their main duty, of course, was to keep the light going, and lighthouse keepers had to get up at least once during the night to tend the light. By growing vegetables, hunting ducks, and catching fish and lobsters, they ate a hearty and varied diet. Some families even kept a cow, chickens, a pig, sheep, and goats for fresh milk, eggs, and meat. Animals also provided companionship. Dogs and cats were common lighthouse pets.

Not all children of lighthouse keepers were taught at home by their parents. If there were enough students at a particular light station, a teacher might be brought in to hold classes for them. Some keepers' children boarded with families in town so that they could attend regular schools. If the family lived on an island, they might row to and from the mainland each day for school.

Elin's stint as temporary lighthouse keeper was not without precedent. In some now-famous instances, children were called upon to assume the duties of lighthouse keeper when their parents were unable to.

Perhaps most famous of the lighthouse children was Ida Lewis, whose father had a stroke soon after accepting his post as keeper of Lime Rock Light in Newport, Rhode Island, in the mid-1800s. Ida assumed many of his responsibilities, including rowing her brother and sister to school in town each day and conducting many rescues. When she was just sixteen, she rescued four young men in their sailboat. They were humiliated at being saved by a young girl. Ida became so well known for her heroism and dedication that President Ulysses S. Grant visited her at the lighthouse in 1869.

The story of Elin's rescue as an infant was based on an actual event that occurred in 1875 at Hendrick's Head Light; and the Flying Santa, who visited young Elin, brought holiday cheer to real lighthouse families beginning in the late 1920s. Maine floatplane pilot Bill Wincapaw had spent years transporting sick or injured islanders to the mainland, and he relied on the lighthouse beacons along the coast to help him navigate. He felt much gratitude to the keepers and wanted to show his appreciation. One Christmas day, he loaded a dozen packages into his plane and dropped them to area lighthouse families. In each package were items like gum, cigarettes, cigars, candy, balloons, rubber balls, dolls, pocket-edition books, razor blades, and puzzles. He first buzzed the lighthouse to alert the keeper that the package was coming, then he returned to drop the bundle.

The packages were so popular that Captain Wincapaw expanded his route, but during World War II the holiday flights were cut back. After the war, the flights resumed, and the Flying Santa, with a little help from friends, including Edward Rowe Snow, covered 115 lighthouses and Coast Guard stations from Massachusetts to the Canadian border.

The holiday visits continue today to lights that are used for Coast Guard housing, organized by a group of volunteers known as the Friends of the Flying Santa.

World War II affected lighthouse families such as Elin's in more dramatic ways. During air raids, when enemy aircraft were thought to be approaching to drop bombs, lights in the area were immediately extinguished and were not relit until the all-clear signal was given. Some lighted navigational aids were darkened, shielded, or dimmed for the duration of the war because they aided enemy vessels. Submarines might use the lights to determine where to lay mines or spot vessels at night when the lighthouse beams silhouetted the ships. By dimming the lights, surface craft were able to see the lights for several hundred yards, but planes flying above 1,000 feet were not able to see them.

In all, 808 lights on the Atlantic and Gulf coasts were temporarily extinguished, including the Statue of Liberty's torch.

It's not certain whether Elin and Dan would have heard German U-boats as early as August 1941, as in this story, but in January 1942, the men in the Cape Henry light station heard a dull rumble as the tanker *Rochester* exploded and sank, the victim of a U-boat attack. The next month, another tanker was torpedoed near the station.

Elin and Dan would, however, have been able to get a glimpse of President Franklin Roosevelt. A secret meeting did take place between Roosevelt and British Prime Minister Winston Churchill in the North Atlantic in August 1941. The two leaders discussed strategies to defeat the Nazis and control of the postwar world. They signed a document that came to be known as the Atlantic Charter. On a chilly August 25 in Rockland, Maine, newsmen waited for Roosevelt to return.

By the 1940s, most lighthouses were already electrified, meaning that Elin's light would have been one of the last remaining without electricity. Today, lighthouses are under the jurisdiction of the Coast Guard, and all are automatic. The only continuously manned lighthouse in the country, the USCG Light Station in Boston, has not been automated because of its historical significance.

Many of the light stations that are no longer operative now serve as museums, inns, or youth hostels. Various lighthouse preservation societies raise money to repair and restore old lighthouse buildings and to create lighthouse parks and museums. These volunteers want to be sure that historic lighthouses survive to be appreciated by future generations.